The Next Chapter

The Next Chapter

Melanie Young

This book is a work of fiction. Names, characters, places, and incidents either are products of the author's imagination or are used fictitiously. Any resemblance to actual events or locales or persons, living or dead, is entirely coincidental.

 To contact the author: mybooks64@gmail.com.

ISBN 978-0-557-39082-3
Second Edition

ACKNOWLEDGEMENTS

Where do I start? OK, first of all I want to thank my mother, Claire Bardwell, who proofread for me. If you find any errors, it's because I either didn't change something she caught, or I added something in after she proofread. Your help is so appreciated, Mom!

Next, Marie McElen, Kristine Pitocchelli and TJ Gallant, thank you all for your suggestions and comments. They were all considered and then thrown out – no, they were very much appreciated! You've helped make this a better novel. TJ, you have a bright future ahead in the editing world!

Also, Claire Cook, author of *Must Love Dogs*, thank you for the inspiration and advice. You have been helpful and kind ever since I first emailed you last July. I was so glad I got to meet you in person at Bookmania in Stuart. Yvonne Mason, author of Silent Scream, thank you for all the advice and guidance you have given me. It was great that I happened to go to your workshop in Jupiter because you have become a wonderful friend and mentor to me.

To my sons, Donovan Young and Anthony Young, thank you for listening to me talk about this story for the past six months as though you were interested. It doesn't matter whether you were really interested or not, because you seemed interested, and that's all I needed.

And finally, to my husband Dean, thank you for not objecting when I invited the characters of The Next Chapter into our lives and home, to live with us six months ago. Thank you for listening to me talk about The Next Chapter ever increasingly since I started writing it. Thank you for not objecting when I finally decided to follow my dream!

For my parents
Sidney and Claire Bardwell
married 50 years
August 6, 2010

Chapter One

It was another cloudy and rainy day in Northwest Oregon. The fog was sitting just above the tops of the trees, hiding the mountains under the gloom. The temperature was cool, and the moisture in the air made it seem colder than it was. The rain was coming down in sheets; visibility was terrible.

Carol had cancelled the appointment for her afternoon sitting with Monica and David, a newly engaged couple, who had insisted their engagement photo be taken at the park where he had proposed to her. It just wasn't possible to keep the couple, the equipment, and herself dry. Nor was it possible to get the proper lighting under this dark, dreary sky. The bride-to-be was disappointed, but there was no option unless they were willing to have the sitting at her studio. After locking up the studio, Carol drove the four blocks to her empty home.

Carol hated days like this. It was difficult not to think about that fateful day in May four years ago that had changed her life so terribly. This was exactly the kind of weather that had caused the accident that took Jim from her. Carol's husband, Jim, had gone to Cannon Beach to visit his Uncle Fred, and while driving home on Highway 26, a driver coming the other way lost control of his vehicle due to the torrential rain, and hit Jim's car head-on. Jim had been killed instantly, as were the three people in the car that hit him. Carol sat in her favorite chair as the terrible memory came back to her, sobbing alone in the dark.

♥

That horrific day, the worst day of her life, had started out wonderfully. Carol had slept in, and Jim woke early, which was unusual for both of them. After reading the morning paper, taking a shower, and pulling on his favorite weekend jeans and a University of Oregon sweatshirt, he cooked breakfast for Carol and surprised her with breakfast in bed. He made a ham and cheese omelet, bacon, toast and orange juice. Carol woke to see Jim walking through the bedroom door, carrying the breakfast tray. Jim added a beautiful yellow rose, which he had cut from Carol's rose bush outside the back door, to the breakfast tray before bringing it in to her. He set the tray on her bedside table and kissed her gently. She stretched and smiled up at her husband of nearly 26 years, her high school sweetheart. She was as much in love with him as she had been all those years ago.

"What did I do to deserve breakfast in bed?" Carol asked.

Jim slid open the drapes of the door to their balcony. "You don't have to do anything, my dear. You did the best thing you could ever do for me when you married me. You always deserve the best," Jim answered. "I love you so much! Can you believe our 26th anniversary is only a month away? It seems like we were newlyweds just yesterday. I can't wait for the cruise."

"I love you, too! I still can't believe you planned the cruise without telling me, and that you managed to keep it a secret for so long. What an awesome way to celebrate our anniversary. I'm the luckiest woman in the world to have you for a husband." Carol took a bite of the bacon. Jim always overcooked everything, but Carol loved him and could overlook the fact that he was a terrible cook, especially since he so rarely cooked. She quickly took a bite of the omelet, trying to disguise her distaste for the *charcoal* bacon. It had been so thoughtful of him to make breakfast for her. She usually just had some fruit or yogurt, so this was definitely a nice surprise.

Jim watched her, knowing she didn't like the bacon, and loving her more for not complaining about it. "I really wanted to keep the cruise a secret and surprise you when the time came. But I knew with our anniversary being in the heart of the busy season with your business, you wouldn't be able to get away if I didn't give you time to plan well in advance." He

Carol drank some of the orange juice; at least he couldn't mess up pouring orange juice from the carton. "It's nice that Sarah is such a great assistant. I was lucky to find her. Without an assistant, it would have been impossible to take this trip. Who knew when we chose to get married in the month of June that I would end up as a wedding photographer, making me always busy around our anniversary?" She smiled and Jim. "I'm so glad you planned this. After all these years, this will be our first anniversary to actually spend the day together, and we get 10 whole days."

Carol had a full day of photography booked. She had a wedding at 10:00 and another at 3:00. Both weddings were large, so she would be busy. "What are you going to occupy yourself with today, Jim?" Carol asked.

"I'm going to head over to Cannon Beach and visit Uncle Fred," Jim replied. "He sounded down in the dumps when I called him last week, so I thought a walk on the beach would do him good. I'll take him to lunch. He always enjoys the salmon quiche from Lazy Susan Café. I worry about Fred. When Aunt Margaret passed away, his heart was buried with her."

"He needs you. With your cousin so far away and Margaret gone, you are all he has now. It will be good for both of you to spend the day together," Carol told Jim. "I would love to see Fred too, but I will go with you next time."

"Yes, we should try to get over to see him together before we leave for the cruise if we can."

Carol thought for a moment. "Why don't we go after the cruise when Andrea will be visiting and we can take her with us?" Andrea was Jim and Carol's only child, who moved to Florida with her best friend after they graduated high school to attend FAU. Carol suddenly noticed the time and said, "I need to get my rear in gear. My first wedding is in two hours and I haven't even showered." Carol rose from the bed and glanced out through the window across the balcony, "Wow, the sun is shining, and hardly a cloud in the sky. It looks like a great day for a walk on the beach. I'm jealous but happy you and Fred are getting out and will be able to enjoy such a nice day at the ocean.

You should probably get moving too. Does Uncle Fred know you're coming?" Carol was walking into the bathroom as she spoke.

"Yes, I called him before I cooked breakfast. You're right, I better hit the road. By the way, I didn't have time to clean up after cooking breakfast. Sorry!" Jim said, sheepishly. "I'll call you before I head back this evening." Jim followed Carol to the bathroom door, wrapping her in his arms and giving her a kiss. "Have a wonderful day, sweetheart." Jim hurried down the stairs and out to the garage. He decided to take the convertible since the weather was good.

Carol smiled as she stepped into the shower. Jim had given her such a fantastic surprise with breakfast in bed, but she would have a messy kitchen to come home to after working all day. He would never change. He had always created chaos when cooking. Maybe she should work on teaching him how to be neater in the kitchen. It wouldn't be easy, but neither was cleaning up after him.

♥

The nice weather held throughout the day. Even though both had been indoor weddings, as almost all are in the Portland area in May, Carol always took some of the pictures outside; the bride and groom exiting the church, the tossing of the bouquet, and driving away in the garishly decorated car. She was thoroughly exhausted. When she finally left the second wedding, she noticed the clouds had moved in. Carol was glad she had insisted on finding a location for her studio that was close to home since she needed to drop off her equipment. As she pulled up in front of the studio, a few raindrops started to fall.

Carol hurried to get the equipment into the studio. Just as she was finishing, and ready to lock up, her cell phone rang. She reached into her purse, pulling her phone out, "Jim?"

"Hi, Babe, how was your day?"

"It was great, and both weddings were fabulous, but now I am totally pooped," Carol answered, as she was locking the door. "Did you have a good visit with Fred?"

Jim replied, "It was a great day. Uncle Fred really needed it. He has been cooped up for too long. His friends come by to see him, but I don't think any of them are successful at getting him to go anywhere. I'm glad I got him out of the house. The weather was perfect, the ocean was beautiful, and the salmon quiche was delicious as always! You were right. It was good for both of us. Fred is looking forward to seeing you when we go next time. When I mentioned Andrea possibly coming to visit, his eyes lit up. I hope we can make that happen."

"I'm looking forward to it as well! I haven't seen Fred since Christmas," Carol responded, as she started her car. "Jim, the rain is picking up here. Is it raining on that side of the mountain?"

"Yes, it started sprinkling about 30 minutes ago, and I think it will continue all night. I put the top up on the convertible before I left Uncle Fred's house. The sky is pretty dark. I'm just getting to

Sunset Highway, Carol, so I will probably lose service in a couple minutes."

"Drive careful, Jim. I will see you when you get home. I love you."

Jim smiled, "I love you, too, sweetheart. I'll see you in about an hour and a half." He lost signal before the last word was out of his mouth.

Carol pulled into the garage, and remembered the huge mess Jim left for her in the kitchen. "If I didn't love that man so much, and if it wasn't so sweet of him to make me breakfast in bed, I would kill him for leaving such a mess for me to clean up," she said aloud to herself as she set her purse on the kitchen counter and surveyed the disarray before her. She had no idea how Jim managed to dirty so many dishes just cooking breakfast for the two of them.

Carol looked around the kitchen, and glanced at the clock. It was almost 7, and Jim would probably be home by 8:30. After cleaning the kitchen, Carol poured a glass of wine and put her favorite CD on. She sat down to read and enjoy her wine, thinking about the cruise she and Jim would be taking next month as she opened her book.

Carol woke up, startled that she had actually fallen asleep. She glanced at her watch, and it was nearly 9. She worried a little, but figured Jim had stopped to help someone; maybe someone had a flat tire. Jim was always helping people in need. Carol dialed Jim's cell phone to check on him, but there was no answer. She tried to tell herself that he just couldn't answer while helping change a tire, or he wasn't back in an area where he could get cell phone signal yet, but she suddenly got a terrible feeling she couldn't shake. Carol called her neighbor, Joan, who came right over.

Carol opened the kitchen door, just as Joan was walking up. "I know I'm being silly, but I just can't shake this feeling. Thank you so much for humoring me, Joan. I couldn't face waiting alone for some reason."

"Don't you worry about it, sweetie. You know I don't! It's perfectly normal for you to be concerned about Jim. Tell me about the plans for the cruise." Joan wanted to take Carol's mind off her distress. "I'll make us some tea."

"Thank you, Joan. You are such a great neighbor and friend." Carol sat down and started telling Joan about the plans for their Caribbean cruise. It almost took her mind off worrying about Jim. "After we get back from the cruise, Andrea is coming for a visit. She is bringing her boyfriend. I have a feeling she will have a ring on a certain finger. She has been on the verge of telling me something and then stops herself, and says she will tell me later. She can't fool her mom!"

Just then, there was a knock on the door. Carol face was suddenly ashen as she looked at Joan. "I'll get it, Carol." Joan opened the door and they saw an Oregon State Trooper standing there.

Chapter Two

The sun was shining, and clouds were sparse in the beautiful blue sky. Carol had just snapped the last picture for Monica and David's sitting. It was a gorgeous park, and she understood why David had chosen such a lovely setting to propose, and why they wanted to have their engagement photos done here. She thought back to the day Jim had proposed to her at Manito Park in Spokane on Thanksgiving Day during her senior year in high school. "Carol, we picked a date for the wedding," Monica interrupted her thoughts. "It's only a few months away. I hope you can do our photography!"

"I'll check my schedule. What's the date?" Carol asked Monica.

"September 5th. It's the first Saturday in September. I know that's really soon, but we have reasons why we need to have the wedding right away. Oh…I just realized how that sounded…and that's not why," she giggled. "We just heard that David's brother, his best man, is shipping out to Afghanistan in October so we wanted to have the wedding before he leaves. You're the best wedding photographer I have ever seen. I love your work. I hope you can do our wedding."

Carol was checking her appointments in her Blackberry as Monica was talking. She looked into Monica, seeing the emotions on her face, "I do have a wedding scheduled that morning. What time is your wedding?"

Monica was nearly jumping up and down with excitement. "We are having an evening wedding. It's at 5! Can you do it?" Monica asked, grabbing Carol's arm.

Carol smiled at Monica's enthusiasm. She was so much like Andrea. "Yes, I can! I'll put your wedding in my books right now. We need to get together to go over the specifics, and I'll call you tomorrow to set that up."

♥

Her appointment with Monica and David this afternoon had brought back so many memories for Carol. As she was driving back to the studio, she couldn't help but reminisce about her life with Jim. It had been love at first sight for her. Jim Davison was so handsome. His face would have been almost perfect had it not been for his crooked nose and the scar on his left eyebrow which made him look like he was always surprised. His nose had been broken when he was in the eighth grade. He had been hit by a baseball during a game. The scar on his eyebrow was from a bicycle accident when he was nine.

Jim and Carol had first met in Spokane, Washington, while they were both attending Rogers High School. Carol was just beginning her freshman year and Jim was a junior. Carol's mother had been hesitant to allow Carol to date a boy who was two years older than she, but since Jim was so polite and truly a gentleman, Maggie had given in. For the next two years the young couple had been nearly inseparable. Jim graduated from high school two years before Carol, and had gone to University of Oregon, continuing their relationship long distance.

Two years later, after Carol graduated from Rogers, they were married. Jim had proposed during his Thanksgiving break from college when Carol was a senior. As a wedding gift, Jim's parents had put a generous down payment on the home Jim and Carol would live in together for the next 26 years in Tigard, Oregon.

♥

Carol pulled into the parking lot of Enchantments, her studio, which was a remodeled small Victorian style house, and walked in. The house had been converted to a duplex style building. She shared the building with Floral Fantasy, a flower shop owned by Nathan and Mary Johnson. It was a great combination as they were able to gain business from each other. "How did the sitting go?" Sarah asked, as Carol set down her camera bag.

"Great! Monica and David have set the date. That reminds me, I need to sync my Blackberry before we close. I don't want to overbook!"

"Did you hear there is a videographer moving in on this block? This has definitely become the destination location for weddings!" Sarah exclaimed. Besides Enchantments and Floral Fantasy, there was a jewelry store, a wedding stationery business, a wedding planner and a caterer on the same block.

"Yes, I have known Robert for a few years. We have done many of the same weddings. I'm glad he is moving nearby. It's great for all of our businesses," Carol responded, as she was plugging her Blackberry into her computer. "Not that we are hurting for business."

Sarah replied, "That's true. I learned so much in the first two years I worked for you. Now that I have worked here five years, I am seriously considering your offer to buy in as partner. Being so busy has definitely helped me learn the business quickly. You've been so good to me."

"You've been a Godsend to me," Carol shot back. "Business has been so good that if you hadn't been here, and if you hadn't been the best assistant I could imagine, I don't know what I would have done."

It was closing time, and both women had been tidying up for the day when the phone rang and Sarah answered. Carol could tell from hearing Sarah's part of the conversation that it was a new mother interested in booking them for christening photos. Even though she had begun her business doing only wedding photos, babies were becoming her favorite subjects.

As they walked out the door a few minutes later, and Carol locked up, Sarah asked, "Do you have any plans tonight? I am having some people over, and I know this is last minute, but I would love it if you would join us."

"Is this another attempt at match-making? You know I am not interested. Nobody can replace Jim! Actually I am tired and I am looking forward to relaxing with a good book and an even better glass of wine."

"The offer stands if you change your mind later. I know you can't replace Jim, I just don't want you to be lonely."

"My dear, I don't have time to be lonely." This wasn't true, but Carol always put up a brave front. She was increasingly lonely, which is why she worked harder all the time.

♥

Carol sat in her kitchen that evening eating a salad for dinner, alone as usual. There was a knock at the kitchen door and Carol knew it was her neighbor, Joan. Joan had been a dear friend and neighbor since she and Jim moved in 30 years ago. "The door's open, Joan." Carol shouted. "You know you don't need to knock," she stated as Joan came in the door.

"I just don't want to startle you," Joan said as she closed the door and looked over at Carol. "You look tired. You have been working too hard. You work harder al the time. You need to remember there is more to life than just working. How was your day?"

Carol sighed, "It was busy. I am grateful to have Sarah there. She told me today she has been giving thought to my offer to have her buy in as a partner."

"I'm glad to hear that! Maybe you won't work so hard if you can't tell her to go home. You know she is willing to do more around there even now."

"I know, Joan, I just feel bad because she has a husband at home she needs to spend time with. I wish I would have spent more time with Jim. I don't want Sarah to make the same mistakes."

"There was no way for you to know that you and Jim wouldn't grow old together. You were both working hard to prepare for your future, a future you both expected to share. It was a tragedy that took him from you. Don't blame yourself for not spending more time with him. You know Jim wouldn't want you to blame yourself…you know he would want you to be happy. He always used to say that he wanted the best for you and that you deserved to be happy, and you know he meant it." Joan looked lovingly at Carol. She was like a daughter to her. After pausing to carefully choose her words, Joan advised, "You have to move on at some point. I know you miss Jim, and you don't know how to live without him. But, honey, Jim died four years ago, and he wouldn't want you to live the way you have been. He would want you to be happy. You need to learn how to live without him. You won't, and shouldn't, ever forget him but he wouldn't want you to stop living because he isn't here."

"Joan, that's just ridiculous, I haven't stopped living. I get up and go to work every day."

"I know you do. But work is the only thing you do. You have no life outside of your business. Please just give some thought to what I have been saying."

"I will, Joan, but really I'm very busy with Enchantments."

"That's my point! You do nothing but work! There is room for more in your life even when your business is thriving."

Carol knew what Joan was saying to her was right, but she didn't want to admit it. Even more, she didn't want to change it. She was still mourning Jim. "I'm not going to argue with you, Joan, but I just don't know how I would fit anything else in my schedule."

"I'm not going to argue with you either, Carol. Look around you…you have been home for an hour and I would be willing to bet this house is spotless, so now that you are done with dinner, you have plenty of time on your hands. You could be using some of this time to *live.* I know you better than you think. I probably know you better than you know yourself these days. I know how you spend your time at home. You clean…or you work on your business matters. You manage your business better than most. You don't manage you life at all.

"You're still young. If it wasn't for the fact that I come by most evenings, you would spend every night alone after work. Think about whether you want to spend the rest of your life watching TV alone in the evenings."

"Well, I do work evenings sometimes, Joan. And Sarah invited me over for dinner this evening, and I would have accepted her offer but she was trying to do some match making, and I am not ready for that. I don't think I will ever be ready to date. For that matter, Joan, maybe you should practice what you preach. I haven't seen you dating a bunch of men."

"I wasn't talking about you dating. I was only saying…"

The phone rang, interrupting Joan. As Carol reached for the phone she glanced at the caller id and her face lit up, "Oh, it's Andrea!"

"Give Andrea my love. I will catch up with you later," Joan whispered as she walked to the door. She opened the door and turned to wave as she closed it softly. Joan hoped it would be a long conversation.

Carol missed Andrea more in the four years since Jim had been gone than she had in the first couple years Andrea had lived in Florida. Carol exclaimed, as she answered the phone, "Andrea, sweetie, how are you?"

"I'm doing great, Mom. How are you? Are you ready for a visit from your favorite daughter and son-in-law?"

Carol was beaming now, "Of course I am! I'm always ready for a visit from you and Jason. When are you coming?"

"We are online right now and we can get a flight next Thursday if that isn't too soon for you. We were thinking of staying a week."

"Wonderful!" Carol was elated to hear her daughter and son-in-law would be coming to visit. She had gone to Florida to see them at Christmas, but hadn't seen them since then, and they hadn't been to Oregon for over a year. "What's bringing you to Portland?"

"You are, Mom! We miss you and we haven't been to see you since we came up for Nana's 70th birthday. This time we're not going to Spokane though. This visit is just to see you. Well, maybe while you're at work, we might take a ride over to see Uncle Fred one day."

Carol poured a glass of wine as they talked. Andrea filled her in on how her husband, Jason, was doing with his accounting firm and how she was doing as an aerobics instructor at the gym where she worked. Carol told Andrea how her business was doing. They talked for over an hour but it seemed like just a few minutes.

"I hate to end the call, Mom, but it's almost 11 here, and I have a 5 am class to teach. I should get to bed. Jason booked the flight and a rental car while we were talking. We should get to your house around 7 or 7:30 next Thursday."

"I'm so glad you called. You made my day. What am I saying? You made my week! I can't wait to see you!"

"Me too! Oh…Mom?"

"Yes?"

"Don't go to any trouble. Let us take care of you this time!"

♥

Carol was ecstatic! She had to tell someone. She walked over to Joan's house. As she was tapping on the door, she opened it and peaked in. Joan was talking on the phone, but she smiled and waved Carol in. "I'm looking forward to it, Martin, I'll see you tomorrow," Joan said, as she set the phone down.

"Who's Martin?"

Chapter Three

Andrea placed the phone down, and smiled at her husband, Jason. "Mom is excited to see us. She'll be even more excited when she hears our great news! I just hope we can convince her to move to Florida this time. She always says she can't leave her business. But I happen to know that her assistant, Sarah, is seriously thinking about taking her up on the offer to buy into the business. Maybe Sarah would even buy Mom out. If she wanted to, Mom could start up a new photography business here in Florida."

Jason stood up and walked over to Andrea, taking her in his arms and said, "Don't get your hopes too high, Andy. I want your mom to move here too, but I just don't want to see you disappointed if she won't move." He kissed her forehead and held her tighter.

"How can she not, Jace? She *has* to move here. Her only daughter is going to have a baby and give her the first grandchild. Once she finds out about the baby, I just know she will want to be here!" They stood silently looking out across the Atlantic Ocean from the balcony of their condo for several minutes, immersing themselves in the magic of the moment.

♥

"Carol, did you have a nice talk with Andrea?"

"Yes, I did! Oh, I'm so excited, Joan! Andrea and Jason are coming for a visit. They are flying in next Thursday and staying a week. I can't wait to see them! I wish they could have given me more notice so I could clear my calendar but I'm sure Sarah won't mind if I ask her to do a little more while they are here. So, by the way...who's Martin?" Carol asked again.

"That *is* exciting! I'm so pleased to know they are coming to visit. You need that diversion. It's almost like they knew what we were talking about before Andrea called you."

"Are you avoiding my question? I've asked twice who Martin is and you still haven't answered." Carol sat down at the kitchen table across from Joan.

Joan chuckled, "Martin is a friend I met at Bingo. He and I had run into each other several times at the bingo hall and enjoyed each other's company, so we started arranging to go at the same time rather than leaving it to chance. We went to lunch last weekend and had a nice time. He called tonight and asked me if I would like to go to lunch again tomorrow. His wife passed away about three years ago and he now is getting on with his life, unlike some people I know," Joan nodded toward Carol. "It's been good for both of us to talk to each other about our memories of Ralph and Martin's wife, Liz. Liz had cancer also. It's a common bond we share and we have an understanding when we are talking to each other that most other people he and I know don't have.

"That brings me back to our earlier conversation, Carol, when you said you haven't seen me dating. I guess I really don't date in the traditional sense of the word. But over the past year or two there are a few gentlemen I have met at church, or through friends that I have spent time with, mostly lunches. I haven't discussed them because none of them were important enough to talk about. Sometimes when I've mentioned lunch with a friend, it's a male friend. Martin is different than the other men, and I think there is a possibility of our friendship developing into something more. If I can move on at my age, sweetie, you can too."

"I want to meet Martin."

"Well, let's see how things go, and then I definitely want you to meet him. But let's get back to you." Joan reached across the table and took Carol's hands in hers. She looked into her eyes and said, "Carol, I was serious about what I said earlier. It's just not healthy for you to bury yourself in your work, and do nothing else. I know you miss Jim, and I know it's hard for you to live without him, but it's time for you to try."

"But Joan…"

"I don't want to hear it, Carol. I want you to listen to what I'm telling you. You know that what I've been telling you is the same thing Jim would tell you if he could. If you honestly think about it, you know I'm right. You have to move on. I'm not talking about diving in head first without a care in the world. I just think it's time for you to get your feet wet, to test the waters." Joan paused for a moment letting Carol absorb some of what she had said. "When you're reading a great book, and something tragic happens, you don't put the book down, never to pick it up again. You turn the page and read the next chapter. It's time you moved on to *your* next chapter. It's time to turn the page."

♥

After the guests left for the evening, Tom helped Sarah with the clean-up. Sarah's husband, Tom, was a successful real estate broker, who managed a large real estate office. "Tom, I made an appointment with George at the bank to talk about a business loan as we discussed. I hope you can come with me. Buying into Enchantments will be a big investment for us, and I want you to be involved with this part of it."

"Of course, darling, when is the appointment? As long as it fits into my schedule, I will be there."

"I made the appointment for eight on Wednesday morning. I thought that would be best for both of us. George said the bank isn't open that early, but he'll meet with us at the studio instead."

"That's perfect. I don't have anything scheduled on Wednesday until noon. I think this is a great move."

"I'm so fortunate I was able to get this job with Carol after I graduated," Sarah stated.

"That's true," Tom agreed. "You're a talented photographer, but I know it's been helpful to you that you were able to apprentice with her. Now, do you have anything planned for the weekend?" Tom put his hands on her narrow waist.

"Carol and I have a wedding tomorrow at one. After that, I thought it would be nice to drive over to Seaside and maybe spend the night at that cute bed and breakfast we stayed at last time. What do you think?"

"Fantabulous!" Tom said, kissing her neck. "I'll call them in the morning and make the reservation. How about checking in upstairs now?"

Chapter Four

"That was a beautiful wedding. Sometimes the smaller more intimate ceremonies are the nicest," Carol said as she and Sarah loaded the camera equipment into the back of her pearl white Lexus RX. She started the engine and headed back to the studio.

"It does stand out among all the weddings I have seen since I started working for you," Sarah agreed. "I'm so excited for you that Andrea is coming to visit! It will be a busy week for both of us. Tom and I are meeting with our banker on Wednesday to see about getting a loan to buy in as partner."

"That's terrific, Sarah! I can't tell you how glad I am that you are taking me up on my offer. I'd like to meet with you and Tom before your meeting with the banker so we can go over figures and I can give you copies of the finances the banker will probably need to have."

"Great! Come to our house for dinner on Monday night and we can go over things." Sarah was thoughtful for a moment as she was thinking about what to serve. "I'll ask Tom to grill some salmon. Oh, did I tell you that Tom and I are driving over to Seaside this afternoon? We're staying at this great B and B we found last time we went there, Gilbert Inn."

"Monday night it is, Carol exclaimed. "You two have fun in Seaside. It's such a nice little town…I haven't been there since Jim died. I've been over to see Jim's uncle in Cannon Beach, but not to Seaside." Carol was thoughtful for a moment with memories of Jim. They used to enjoy their weekends on the beach, and Seaside had been one of their favorite places. She interrupted her own thoughts, "Oh, I forgot to tell you that I've decided to hire a new assistant. Now that you are going to be my partner, we'll need another employee and now, as partner, you have to help me make decisions," she said with a smile. "I posted a notice at Portland Community College for their photography students to apply, as I did when I hired you." Carol was pulling into the studio parking lot. The women walked around to the back of the SUV to unload the equipment.

Sarah asked, "Do you really think there is enough work to support another assistant, Carol?"

Carol opened the door of the studio and they walked in, setting their loads on the counter. "You'll see when we go over the books. We can definitely afford to hire another employee. We'll talk about it when I come over Monday evening. Now scoot! Get out of here!" Carol waved her arms toward the door. "You need to get going. You and Tom have a nice time in Seaside. I will put everything away here. Go, go, go."

♥

Carol arrived home feeling anxious; she had been giving a lot of thought to Joan's comments about getting on with her life. The advice Joan had given her was what had prompted her to move forward with hiring a new assistant. She knew Joan was right, but she was scared and apprehensive about moving on. She really had no idea how to begin. She had grown so accustomed to her life with Jim, and now after four years of not living her life, she didn't know how to start to create her own life again.

Before Jim had been killed, they had both enjoyed a very active social life. They hosted dinner parties frequently and attended gatherings often with their many friends. After Jim's death, Carol had turned down their friends' invitations so often that she now rarely received any.

Carol realized she had put aside all of the interests she had in the past. When she wasn't working, she was home ether cleaning or planning ways to improve her business. She had managed to visit her daughter and son-in-law in Florida from time to time. Her neighbor, Joan, was her main source of companionship now. "Jim, what should I do? I need your guidance?" she said aloud. Instantly, an idea came to her. Carol picked up her phone and called Joan.

"Joan, are you busy? Have you eaten dinner?"

"No, I'm not and no, I haven't. Why do you ask?" Joan replied, with a smile in her voice.

"I want to treat you to dinner. I haven't gone out to dinner in a long time and I thought tonight would be a great time to change that. I was hoping you would like to go with me."

Joan even brighter now, "I would love to, dear. I'll walk over there in about 20 minutes if that suits you." This was a great indication that her little talk with her friend had done some good. She was pleased to see Carol at least making this small step.

Carol changed into a pair of black slacks and her favorite pink sweater, ran a brush through her hair, and swiped some lipstick on her lips. She was just grabbing a light jacket from the hall closet when Joan tapped on the kitchen door and walked in.

"Joan, I was thinking we could go to Red Lobster. Sound good to you?" Carol asked.

Joan gave Carol a big hug. "That sounds absolutely perfect to me, sweetie. You know I love seafood. I'm pleased that you invited me to dinner…but more than that, I'm excited you're getting out of your house to do something other than work!"

♥

The ladies arrived at the restaurant and, being a Saturday night, they were told they would have a 30 minute wait for a table. The maitre d' handed them a pager, "You can wait in the lounge if you would like to have a drink while you wait."

Carol and Joan chose a table in the lounge near the fireplace and both ordered a glass of wine. Even though the restaurant was crowded, people seemed to be speaking in low tones, so it was not noisy. The atmosphere was perfect for a dinner between two old friends. They both liked the table and decided to have their dinner in the lounge instead of waiting.

"How's your lobster?" Carol asked Joan.

"Delicious! I think I've died and gone to heaven. Carol, this is such a nice treat. I hope this means you are making, or at least thinking about, other changes in your life."

"Joan, I wanted to talk to you about that. I was kind of angry with you when you first talked about me moving on "to the next chapter" and getting on with my life. I've thought about it a lot. The reality is, you were right, even though I don't like to admit it. If Jim can see how I have been living my life since he died, I'm sure he isn't happy with me. He would want me to live life for both of us, and he wouldn't want me to spend my life alone. I just don't really know *how* to move forward. I need your help. I'm scared. Until Jim died, I spent my entire adult life with him.

"I do have to say, dinner out was definitely a fantastic first step," Carol suddenly smiled. "I've made steps toward hiring a new assistant since Sarah, and her husband, are talking with their banker about a loan for Sarah to buy in as a partner."

Joan was beaming, "I'm so pleased and so proud of you! My little girl is growing up," she joked. "You said you don't know how to move forward, but you are doing a good job of faking it. You just take one step at a time."

"Or one page at a time," Carol smiled, playing on Joan's original analogy. They got up to leave the restaurant.

"I have a great idea! Since you bought me dinner tonight, let me take you to a movie tomorrow. We can go to a matinee after church," Joan offered.

"I don't know, Joan, I have a lot of cleaning to do since Andrea and Jason are coming on Thursday."

"What cleaning? Your house is always spotless. Let's go to a movie tomorrow. I hear *Duplicity* is good. When was the last time you went to a movie anyway?" Joan asked.

"Hmmm...I don't know...it was with Jim. I think it was that Johnny Depp movie...something about a window...oh, *Secret Window*!" Carol pensively nodded her head. "Yes, that was the last one."

"Well, then it's time to go to a movie. It's supposed to be drizzly and dreary tomorrow, so, my dear, it will be a great day to be in the theater and I am taking you to the movie, and I won't take no for an answer," Joan said as they were getting back into Carol's car.

Chapter Five

"You both look so good. I love it that you surprised me with a visit!" Carol exclaimed as she was hugging Andrea and Jason. "I hope you don't mind, but I asked Joan to join us for dinner. She should be here any minute."

"Of course, we don't mind! Joan is like family," Andrea replied. "Can I set the table for you, Mom?"

"No…the table is already set in the dining room. Sit down you two, you must be tired. It's a long flight from Florida. Can I get you anything to drink? Beer, wine, water…anything?"

"Water is good for me, but let me get it," Andrea answered. "Jason, do you want a beer?"

Joan walked in the kitchen door at that moment and set a bottle of Pinot Noir on the counter. "Looks like I'm fashionably late," she announced. "How are you kids? When did you get here? Did you have a nice flight?" Joan was hugging them both as she asked the questions.

"Which question do you want us to answer first?" Jason laughed. "We just got here about 20 minutes ago, the flight was uneventful, and we're both doing great, never better! And how have you been, Joan?"

"Wonderful, as always! Carol, can I help you with anything?"

"I think I have it all under control. Unless you want to open that beautiful bottle of wine you brought," Carol answered.

Jason picked up the wine, "Let me do that for you. Who would like a glass?"

Carol was getting wine glasses from the cabinet, "Let's all have some."

"None for me," Andrea chimed in. "I'm not drinking any…tonight."

Carol looked at Andrea quizzically, "No wine, I don't think I've ever known you to turn down a good glass of wine."

"I know, Mom. I'm just tired. I'm sure wine would knock me out." Andrea looked over at Jason with a warning not to spill the beans yet.

Carol excused herself to pull the roast from the oven. "Dinner's ready." Everybody sat down to the table and started dishing up. The meal was delicious and the conversation lively as they ate.

"Fantastic meal!" Jason said, as they were all finishing. "You've outdone yourself, Carol. It's great to have a mother-in-law who is such a great cook. Not that you're not a great cook too, Andy." Jason quickly redeemed himself before Andrea could read anything into his statement.

"Thank you, Jason. I love having my family around me. Dinner even tastes better when you have people you love with you."

Jason looked over at Andrea, "That brings up a good point, Carol. One of the reasons Andrea and I took this trip was to ask you, again, to move to Stuart. We want to have you in Florida so you can be nearer to us."

"Yes, Mom, it's really important to me…to us," Andrea said with the hint of a tear in her eye."

Carol looked from Andrea to Jason and back again. "My dears, I would love nothing better than to live close to you. You know I love you both more than words can express, but my life is here in Tigard. This is my home, the home that I have lived in since your father and I got married, Andrea. I've spent 30 years in this house. My business is here. The life I built with Jim is here. I just don't know how many ways to tell you that I love you with all my heart, but I have to love you from here. My life is here."

"Carol," Joan interjected, "at least listen to what they have to say." She arose to clear the table.

"Thank you, Joan," Andrea said. "Mom, we want you to come to Stuart for ten days. We are paying for the trip for your Mother's Day gift. You can't say no because I have already talked to Sarah about it. She told me she could handle everything while you are away. Just come for the visit, and don't make up your mind yet. Please, Mom."

"Sarah didn't say anything to me."

Jason laughed, "Of course not. Andy made her promise not to. Please take the trip and come to Florida. We made all the reservations already; the flight, the rental car, and a nice bed and breakfast. The flight is three weeks from today so that gives you plenty of time to do whatever you need to do to before then."

Joan walked back into the room. "Every book has many chapters," was all she said.

♥

"Sarah, you're a traitor," Carol accused when she walked in the door of Enchantments the following morning. “You didn’t even let on about Andrea and Jason planning for me to go to Florida,”

Sarah looked up and smiled, “Of course I didn’t. I promised Andy I wouldn’t say a word. It’s such a thoughtful thing for them to do for you. I’m glad you were completely taken by surprise!”

Carol sat down and looked directly into Sarah’s eyes, “I’m sure my darling daughter didn’t tell you that their ulterior motive was to try to get me to move to Florida.” Carol watched for a reaction.

Sarah accommodated her with a look of shock, “Andrea didn’t mention anything about that! She just told me they wanted visit for Mother’s Day so they could spoil you rotten.”

“Yes, well, I’ll go on this trip. I wish like crazy my daughter and son-in-law lived near me. But as I told them last night, my life is here.”

♥

Andrea stood up to help Carol clear the table. She and Jason would be leaving for the airport shortly. They had been holding onto their secret throughout their week with her mother and the time to tell her the exciting news was upon them. “Mom, I’ve really enjoyed our visit and I can’t wait for you to come see us in Stuart.”

“I am so glad you and Jason could spend this time here! I love having you both,” Carol said as they loaded the last of the dishes in the dishwasher.

"Jason and I have one more thing we want to tell you before we leave, and I need you to sit down."

Carol's heart jumped into her throat. "What's wrong?" she asked, bringing her hands up to her chest, her heart thumping wildly.

"Nothing's wrong!" Andrea and Jason both said at the once. They looked at each other and laughed.

Jason said, "We didn't mean to scare you. Go ahead, Andy," he softly encouraged his wife.

Andrea smiled and took her mother's hand, "Mom, you're going to become a grandmother in November. I'm six weeks pregnant. I'm due the day after Thanksgiving!"

Carol screamed with delight. She jumped up and grabbed Andrea in her arms, "My baby is having a baby." Carol and Andrea were both crying tears of joy now. "I'm so happy! Why didn't you tell me sooner? Are you feeling ok? Oh, I need to start quilting again. My grandchild needs a quilt! I wish you would have told me sooner so I could have taken you shopping!"

"There's plenty of time for shopping," Jason interjected. "The baby isn't coming for seven more months. I don't think we timed this very well." He looked at his watch and frowned. "It's time for us to leave for the airport. Ladies, dry your tears and you can cry together in a couple weeks in Stuart," he advised.

Joan rushed through the kitchen door just then, "I was afraid I would be too late to say good-bye to you kids." Joan hugged Andrea and Jason, "It was good to see you both. Have a safe trip home." She looked at Andrea and Carol, "Have you two been crying?"

Carol cried, "I'm going to be a grandmother!" She grabbed a tissue and wiped her eyes. "That explains why Andrea hasn't touched a glass of wine this whole week. We're having a baby!"

Another round of hugs was shared by the four in Carol's kitchen. Jason broke it up, "We really need to get to the airport."

With that, they said their last good-bye and ran out the door. Carol and Joan were both silent for a moment, staring at the door and letting the events of the last couple minutes sink in. Joan was the first to break the silence, "Well, that changes everything, doesn't it?"

"Yes..." Carol nodded, blankly. She was thoughtful a moment, then she shook her head and asked, "What do you mean?"

"Another element has been added to your decision about their request that you move to Florida."

Carol turned her head to stare at the door again, "Yes, that changes everything."

Chapter Six

Traffic was light. It was four a.m. and the morning rush to work hadn't started yet. The sky was clear and the day promised to be a pleasant one. Joan was driving Carol to the airport for the daylong flight to Stuart, Florida.

"Joan, I can't thank you enough for getting up early to drive me to the airport. I really didn't want to leave my car in the parking garage for 10 days. I could have taken a taxi, but this is so much nicer," Carol stated. They sat in silence for a moment. "You know, I have given a lot of thought to Andrea and Jason's request for me to move to Florida, and I'm not going to do it. When they first told me about the pregnancy, I was ready to move on the spot. I was so excited to be a grandma and I still am. I've realized that although I never wanted to be a long-distance grandmother, other people do it, and I can too. My life is still here in Oregon."

"Carol," Joan started. "Don't rush making this decision. I would hate to see my dear friend and neighbor move away, but I hope you will think this through more carefully. Andrea is your only daughter. You will be a wonderful grandmother. You know that I have two grandchildren who live in Portland, and three who live in Chicago. I've missed out on so many things in their lives. Sure, I have been able to see them for visits, but I missed out on the school concerts, birthday parties, soccer games and sleepovers at my house just for fun. It would have been so much nicer if all my grandchildren could have lived closer to me. I am fortunate that I've had two of them living close. You only have one daughter, so any grandchildren you'll be blessed with will live in Florida. Make sure you are careful with this decision. Take this opportunity Andrea and Jason have given you to look around and think things over."

Carol was shaking her head, "I would love it if Jason and Andrea could move to Oregon, but I just can't move to Florida. Fortunately, I am doing well, and flying to Florida a few times every year is not a problem. It's not ideal, but that's what I have decided. You've convinced me that I need to do more with my life than I have been. I agree with you to a point, and I know Jim would want me to make more of my life than I have. But I can't leave the home that he and I created together. We bought that house when we first married, and all of our memories are there."

Joan had pulled up to the airport; she gently touched Carol's head, "The memories you shared with Jim are right here. That house is just a building in which you shared many of them. Without that building, your memories are still the same. Think about it." Carol didn't say a word as Joan opened the door and helped get the bags from the trunk. "Have a safe flight, and a wonderful time in Florida!" She hugged her, got back in the car and drove away, leaving Carol to check in and consider her latest words of wisdom.

♥

Carol drove north on Interstate 95 heading to Stuart from West Palm Beach in her rental car, a blue Ford Mustang convertible. Her flight had arrived on time, and she called Andrea to let her know she had landed. The plane landed just before 4 p.m. There had been one only stop in Atlanta, with a short layover. She felt tired from the day long plane flight, but was excited to see Andrea and Jason.

The drive to Stuart was a pleasant one. Although traffic was somewhat heavy, Carol was used to it. The blue sky was clear, and the afternoon was comfortably warm, but Carol chose not to put the top down on the convertible. The drive from West Palm Beach to Stuart took her about 45 minutes, but seemed like much less, as she had been deep in thought during the drive.

Carol pulled up to the bed and breakfast Jason and Andrea had reserved for her, Treasure Coast Paradise Inn, and marveled at the Key West style house with the gorgeous wrap around porch. The grounds were beautifully landscaped with native south Florida vegetation, including hibiscus, lantana and palm trees. She felt like she was in paradise.

She walked inside to check in and as she stepped into the foyer, discovered the interior was every bit as fabulous as the outside. She caught a glimpse of the sitting room before she turned to close the door. The walls were a calming shade of blue with white accents throughout the room. "Welcome to Treasure Coast Paradise Inn. You must be Carol," she heard from the next room. Carol moved into the sitting room reception area, and the woman sitting at a desk there smiled, "How was your drive from West Palm Beach? I understand you're from Oregon?"

"Yes," Carol affirmed, "from the Portland area. I came to visit my daughter and son-in-law who live on Hutchinson Island. The drive was nice." Carol reached across the counter to shake hands with the hostess.

"Welcome to South Florida! I'm Anna. My husband and I own the inn. I'll ask Brian to bring in your bags. Let me show you around the inn. Can I get you some tea or anything?"

"Thank you, Anna. I don't need anything just now. I brought my bags to the porch, but it would be wonderful of Brian to bring them up to my room." She glanced around the room. "This is just beautiful!"

Anna gave Carol a tour, pointing out the common areas and showed her the room where she would be staying. The room had a magnificent four poster bed, private bathroom, and French doors leading to a balcony overlooking the St. Lucie River. The room was decorated in a lovely sage green, and furnished with light rattan.

Brian brought Carol's bags up to the room just as Anna was telling Carol of the breakfast times, and other important housekeeping issues. "Carol, this is my husband, Brian. If there is anything either of us can do for you, let us know."

"Thank you, I will." Anna and Brian closed the door as they walked out. Carol rummaged through her purse for her cell phone. She called Andrea to let her know that she had made it to the bed and breakfast. Andrea asked her to come for dinner, and she told her that she wanted to unpack and freshen up first, and would be over in about an hour.

Unpacking her bags took little time. Carol showered and chose a pair of khaki capris and an emerald colored blouse the same color as her eyes for the evening. Seeing that she still had plenty of time, she picked up her cell phone to call Joan.

"Joan, I wanted to thank you again for driving me to the airport this morning."

"You're quite welcome, my dear. Have you seen Andrea yet?"

"No, I'm going driving over to their condo for dinner. I wanted to call you first to let you know I'm here. This inn is beautiful, and my room is gorgeous. I feel so calm and relaxed that I hardly want to leave the room. I had been a little disappointed not to stay with Andrea and Jason, but this is fantastic."

"That's good to hear, Carol. This trip will do you good. Are you giving the quilt to Andrea tonight?" Carol had made a quilt for the baby in the two weeks she had after Andrea and Jason's visit. She had made the quilt in various shades of white, ivory and cream.

"I certainly am. I hope Andrea likes it."

"Of course she'll love it! Carol, have you reconsidered moving down there?"

"Why do you do that, Joan? We were having a perfectly lovely conversation, and you had to go and start that up again. I have to go." With that, Carol ended the call.

Chapter Seven

"Andrea, dinner was as delicious as you are beautiful," Jason said, before eating his last bite of dessert. Andrea had prepared shrimp scampi, baked potatoes, and a tossed salad for their meal, with Cuban rum cake for dessert.

"I'll have to agree with you on that, Jason," Carol exclaimed. "My daughter certainly is a wonderful cook." She got up to start clearing the table.

Jason stood up immediately, "Sit down, Carol. This is your vacation. I'll clear the table, and you lovely ladies sit and relax. It'll just take me a couple minutes." He cleared the table as Carol and Andrea chatted.

"Thank you, sweetheart. Now I remember why I married you," Andrea joked. "Would you both like a Mojito?" she asked. "I make the best! I use coconut rum and that makes them so delicious. I can't drink it, but at least I can smell it." She walked over to the bar while she was talking, not giving them the opportunity to answer. She set the drinks on the table at the same time Jason returned from the kitchen.

Carol rose and picked up the quilt she had made for the baby. "I brought something for you," she said, handing the quilt to Andrea.

"Mom, this is beautiful!" Andrea exclaimed. "How did you make this so quickly?" She gingerly ran her hand over the quilt, tears forming in her eyes.

"I did nothing else after work for ten or eleven days. I haven't used my sewing machine in so long, I took it in to be serviced, and then I bought a new one so I could make this before coming to Florida. I hope you like it."

"I love it! It's the most beautiful quilt I have ever seen," Andrea said. She unfolded it and spread it across the table to look more closely at Carol's handiwork.

Jason put his arm around Andrea's shoulders and looked at the quilt. "Carol, the quilt is really nice, not that I know anything about quilts, but this one is top-notch. Provisimo!" he said with a smile and a wink. "Thank you."

There was a knock at the door, "That must be Andrew," Jason said as he walked over to open the door. "Come in, Andrew. Have a seat. Can I get you anything?"

"No, I can't stay. I just wanted to drop this quote by. Brad and Angie invited me to come for dinner, so it was convenient to bring this by. I see you have company, so I'll be going. Just look this over and call me tomorrow so I can go over it with you and answer any questions you have."

Andrea jumped up, "Andrew, wait a minute. I want you to meet my mother." Andrea put her hands on Carol's shoulders. "This is my mother, Carol Davison," she said to Andrew. "Mom, Andrew Potter is our neighbor's dad. We buy our auto and home owner's insurance from him. Andrew ran a quote for us on the house we want to make an offer on, which we were just going to tell you about."

Carol stood and extended her hand, "It's a pleasure to meet you, Andrew."

"The pleasure is all mine," Andrew took her hand in both of his. "I can see where Andrea gets her gorgeous green eyes." He was thinking Andrea inherited more than just gorgeous eyes from her mother.

"Thank you, Andrew," Carol said, a slight blush tinting her face. She took her hand back.

"Do you live here in Stuart, Carol?" Andrew asked. He was a striking man, with dark hair and deep brown eyes, his skin a golden tan.

Carol shook her head, "No, I'm from Oregon…Portland…Tigard, actually. And you?"

"I'm a Florida native. I own a small insurance brokerage here in town."

"Of course, Andrea said they buy their insurance from you."

Andrea broke into the conversation, "Mom is here to visit, but we are trying to convince her to move to Stuart. Our baby needs to have a grandmother."

"Stuart is a great place to live, Carol. I hope you decide to move here," Andrew said.

Carol replied, "There's a lot to consider. My home and business are in Oregon. My family is here in Florida."

"Your home and business are replaceable," Jason said. He put his hands on the tops of Andrea's shoulders. "Your family isn't."

"I know it isn't any of my business, but your son-in-law has a good point," Andrew said.

“No, it isn’t your business,” Carol said, and then wished she hadn’t been so rude. “I’m sorry, Andrew. I don’t mean to be rude.”

“No need to apologize, Carol. I’m interrupting your evening, and I am supposed to be next door for dinner, so I’ll get out of your way.” Andrew opened the door, “We’ll talk tomorrow about the policy and then let me know when you want to move forward with it,” he said to Jason and Andrea. “Carol, it was nice to meet you.” With that, he was gone. The group moved into the living room, and sat down.

“Mom, did you blush?” Andrea asked.

“I most certainly did not!”

Andrea giggled, “Ok, live in denial if you must.” She and Jason shared a look, suggesting they had both noticed the blush.

“Tell me about the house,” Carol said, purposefully changing the subject. “I wasn’t aware you were looking at houses.” She put her drink on the coffee table.

“When we were on the plane coming back from seeing you we talked about how we didn’t want to raise our children in a condo. The prices are right for buying, so we decided to start looking immediately and we talked to a Realtor the next day,” Andrea explained. “Oh, Mom, we both love this house. It’s the only house we have looked at that we can’t see anything we want to change. It’s bigger than we need, but we figure that just means we won’t outgrow it,” Andrea said with a laugh. “The architecture is actually similar to the bed and breakfast where you’re staying.

"The family room is so cozy, and as soon as I walked into it, I could picture it decorated for Christmas. I know right where the tree will go. There is a gorgeous fireplace, even though there isn't much need for one on the Treasure Coast. The kitchen is fabulous, and there is a formal dining room, as well as a dining area in the kitchen just like you have. There is a nursery next to the master. The colors are all perfect. We won't have to change a thing."

Carol laughed, "Well, I can tell you don't like it very much."

Andrea and Jason both laughed too. "I guess you can hear how excited we are about this house, huh?" Andrea said.

"It's right on the water, Hooker Cove, with a private dock," Jason broke in, "We won't have to dock the boat at the marina anymore. There's a small beach area, and also a pool and hot tub, and all of them are already fenced so we don't have to worry about that when the baby gets older. The garage is the garage I have always dreamed about, and has plenty of room for all the cars and our toys. It's on over an acre of land, which you just don't see on the Intracoastal."

"Oh, and the guest house," Andrea interjected, "The guest house is beautiful and is bigger and nicer than homes some people I know live in. It makes us feel arrogant buying such a grandiose piece of property, but we are getting such a great buy on this place."

"We are going to have one more look tomorrow before making the offer. We thought you might want to come along," Jason said.

“I’d love to see it,” Carol replied.

Andrea said, “Oh, Mom, you’ll be amazed at this house. Make sure you take special note of the guest house. We thought you could live in it temporarily when…if you move here until you find where you want to live.” Carol tensed up as soon as Andrea said this. She massaged her temples with her fingers, as if she had a headache. Andrea noticed this and was saddened.

Carol stood up, “I think you both need to know that I plan to pay you back for this trip. There are two reasons for this. The first being I don’t want you spending so much money on me when you have a baby on the way and you’re buying a new home, or any time for that matter. The second is that I know you have your heart set on my moving here, but as I’ve said before, my business is in Oregon and more importantly the home I shared with your father is there. My life is in Tigard.”

Andrea was crying now, and she was angered, “What life? You don’t have a life! All you do is work! I’ve talked to Joan and Sarah, and I know!” She was shouting now. “You didn’t marry that house; you married my father. Daddy is dead, Mom. You have to keep living…for you…for me…for my baby. Life cheated me out of walking down the aisle on my daddy’s arm on my wedding day. Don’t cheat me out of sharing this part of my life with my mom.” Andrea paused briefly and added. “My father died four years ago and I was so shocked and deeply saddened to lose him so unexpectedly. I lost my mother that same day because without him, my mother stopped living. I can’t get my father back. He’s gone forever. I want my mama to return to me." Tears were streaming down Andrea's face in rivers. She ran from the room.

Carol was crying now also, and watched Andrea for a moment. As she started to follow her daughter, Jason reached for Carol's arm, and gently turned her to face him. "Carol, I love my wife more than I can tell you. This is important to her. All I ask of you is to please keep an open mind. Don't decide anything until you've honestly given this some thought. Give Stuart a chance...give your daughter a chance. Please." He kissed Carol on the cheek and started out of the room to check in on Andrea. "Excuse me for a minute, Carol."

Carol was speechless. She walked out onto the balcony and stood with her hands on the rail. The things Andrea had said to her, along with the things Joan had been telling her lately mingled in her thoughts. She thought how strange it was that she and her daughter had reversed roles in the awkward exchange that had just occurred where she had been the one to learn from Andrea. She was far too young to experience the reversal of mother-daughter roles.

She couldn't shake the feeling that she had been extremely selfish the past four years. She certainly hadn't seen it that way until Andrea had burst. Of course, Andrea was pregnant, so her emotions were out of control. But if she was being honest with herself, Carol recognized that what Andrea had said was true. She couldn't believe how self focused she'd become. "Jim, I've made a mess of this." She said aloud. "I have to fix the relationship I have with our daughter. You and I are going to be grandparents. I wish to God that you could be here to see our little girl be a mommy, but I promise you, I will be a better mother than I have been lately, and I'll be the best grandmother I can be."

Carol felt ashamed that her daughter practically had to slap her in the face to wake her up to the fact that she hadn't been the mother Andrea deserved, and the mother that she had been before Jim's death. She was determined to make it up to her. She didn't know that she would move to Florida. However, she would do what Jason had asked and give it a chance. She realized that she also owed an apology to Joan.

Walking down the hall toward Andrea and Jason's bedroom, Carol could hear that Jason had managed to console Andrea as she no longer heard her sobs. She was formulating in her mind what she would say to try to mend fences with her daughter. She didn't want to give her any false hope about the possibility of her moving, but she did want to make her aware that she would keep an open mind about the idea. She wanted to find a way to try to make up for the years they had missed since Jim died.

The closer she got to their room, the more ambivalent she was about what she would say. She really needed to choose her words carefully. She needed Andrea to understand how sorry she was for messing things up so badly over the past four years. She would make sure they knew that she would take this time in Florida to really consider their request, but that she wasn't making any promises.

Carol was just outside their bedroom now, and could hear them speaking in whispers. She hesitated for a moment, and then planted a smile on her face before walking into the room, after gently tapping on the open door. "May I interrupt for a minute? I won't be long. I need to get back to the B and B soon. It's been a long day. I just have some things I need to say."

Andrea and Jason were sitting on the edge of the bed. Carol scooted the chair that was nearby over next to the bed facing them.

"I owe you both an apology. I've been stupid and blind and selfish. I was lost in my grief, and didn't acknowledge yours, Andrea. The only way I could deal with my grief was to immerse myself in my business. The business is thriving, my house is always spotless, and the rest of my life, including my family, is neglected. I didn't even recognize that fact, even though Joan has been trying to drill it into my head, until you said it to me, Andrea. There isn't any way to get those years back, but I want you to know how sorry and ashamed I am that I haven't been the mother I should have been. I promise to do better. You are right, Andrea. I owe it to myself, you, and the baby. I also owe it to your father." She stood up and wrapped her arms around her daughter, "I'm so sorry, baby!" They were both crying again, but the feelings were different than they had been earlier.

Jason stood up and put his arms around both his wife and mother-in-law. "I'm going to give you ladies some time to yourselves." He kissed both of them on the cheek and walked out of the room.

Carol and Andrea sat in silence, in a close embrace, for a few moments. Carol broke the silence and their embrace, "Andy, I'm sorry I haven't been there for you, and I'm especially sorry you practically had to kick my ass to wake me up to the fact that I've been unfair to you...and to Jason. I promise to do better. Now, let's go find Jason. I want to talk to both of you, and I should go back to the inn soon. I'm thoroughly exhausted, and you need your rest too."

They both stood and walked down the hall arm in arm. They found Jason on the balcony, sitting and watching the waves under the moonlight. The sky was clear and the stars were bright in the sky, lighting up the ocean and the gentle waves. It was a peaceful night; a stark contrast to what had taken place inside earlier.

"Wow, what a lovely night!" Carol exclaimed, as she and Andrea both stepped out onto the balcony. Jason turned and smiled at his wife and mother-in-law.

"Yes, the moon and the stars are so bright tonight you could almost drive without your headlights," Jason joked. "It is a beautiful night. Did you have a nice talk?"

Andrea took her husband's arm, "We did." She smiled up at him.

Carol said, "I should head back to the bed and breakfast soon. Maybe I'll try out your theory with the headlights, Jason." They all laughed. "I want to talk to you both before I go. I want you to know that what you both said to me this evening has not fallen on deaf ears. I will reconsider moving, but I don't want you to get your heart set on it, Andrea. The only thing I can promise is that while I am in Florida, I will look at Stuart with my eyes, heart and mind open. I do want to share this part of your life. I don't want to be a long distance grandmother. This is a beautiful part of the country. I also don't want to make this decision without careful consideration.

"That being said…I want to see the house with you tomorrow. And then I want to take you both to dinner to celebrate making the offer…or if you decide against it, we'll celebrate family! Another thing…I want to take my daughter shopping on Saturday. We need to look at baby things," Carol said.

Andrea and Jason both reached to hug Carol at the same time. Andrea said, "That sounds great! We arranged to see the house at four and Jason and I both work until shortly before that. Will you be ok until then?"

"Yes, I want to walk over to the historic downtown section of Stuart tomorrow morning. From what I heard at the inn, I could probably spend hours...or even days…down there."

"You'll enjoy that. The shops are awesome. We'll pick you up at the inn tomorrow before we go to the house," Jason said. "Don't think that we forgot Mother's Day! For Mother's Day on Sunday we want to take you out on the boat after church. We thought a brunch on the boat would be nice, and we'll avoid the Mother's Day restaurant crowds. Does that sound ok to you?"

"That sounds perfect," Carol answered. "I'll see you both tomorrow." She hugged them both. "I want to apologize again…can you forgive a pig-headed old fool with no eyes to see with and no ears to hear with all these years?" She asked, quoting Ebenezer Scrooge.

Andrea and Jason laughed, and Andrea said, "Oh Mom, you always did quote movies perfectly! Of course we forgive you. I'm just happy to have you back!"

Carol left and drove on the gently curving road back from Jason and Andrea's condo. She thought about all that had been said tonight, as well as the things Joan had been saying to her over the past few months. She vowed to herself to do her best to reclaim her previous self, and stop living as if she were not living.

♥

"Jason, I'm happy that turned out the way it did. After I said those things to my mom and ran to the bedroom, I was afraid she would leave here immediately, hop on the plane and go back to Oregon tonight."

"You know your mother better than that. She may have lost herself in her grief all these years, but she is a caring and intelligent woman. She loves you and she listened to you," Jason held Andrea, as they both continued to enjoy the moonlit waves.

♥

Carol had just returned to the bed and breakfast. She wanted to call Joan, but was disappointed to see that it was almost eleven. She made a mental note to call her in the morning when she remembered the three hour time difference and called her.

"Hello."

"Joan, it's Carol."

"Carol, I didn't expect to hear from you so soon. Is there something wrong?"

"Joan, I just had to call to apologize. I was so rude when we talked earlier."

"No need to apologize, dear. I was being a busy body. I won't bug you about that anymore."

"You were being a friend, Joan. I appreciate you and your friendship more than I can say. I also wanted to tell you about what happened tonight. Andrea had an outburst and it finally brought me to my senses. She said that she lost her mother when her father died, and she wanted me back. Everything you have been saying to me finally clicked in." Carol explained all that had taken place earlier in the evening. "I thought you deserved to hear about the evening. You also deserve an apology for how crummy I have treated you."

"Carol, I understand. We all grieve in our own way. I'm just glad that things are smoothed over for Andrea and you!"

"Another thing…I have put off making a decision about Florida for nine days. I told them I would keep an open mind and give Stuart a chance, and I am."

Chapter Eight

Carol woke up thinking it was late, with the sun shining brightly through the window and birds singing; a well deserved rest she thought. She stretched and yawned, picking up her watch from the bed stand to look at the time. A few minutes past eight, she couldn't believe she had slept so late. She was normally up around five, never needing an alarm clock. Then, as had happened the day before, she remembered the three hour time difference. It was only five o'clock back home; she hadn't really slept in after all.

Thinking about the episode of the previous evening, Carol wondered how she had been so blind for the past few years to her daughter's needs. She only had one child, and even though she was grown, she was still her baby. Of all she had learned from the exchange they had shared last night, she realized she had to start living more in the present. She couldn't change her past behavior; she could only work on today…and tomorrow.

Carol suddenly felt more excited about life than she had in a long time. She had been wondering what she would do with herself with such a long vacation. Now she thought about the fact that since Jim died, she had not taken any vacations of more than a few days at a time. She had flown here to visit Andrea and Jason a few times, and had taken a couple trips over to Spokane to visit now and then. She never stayed more than a day or two in either case. Other than that, there had only been day trips to Cannon Beach. The business trips to photography seminars didn't qualify as vacations. Andrea and Joan were both right in telling her she hadn't been living, and she intended to change that.

She thought about the day ahead. She was eager to see the house Andrea and Jason wanted to buy, but that was hours away. Historic downtown Stuart was calling her. Carol had heard great things about the shops. She showered and dressed in white shorts and a sleeveless turquoise blouse before going downstairs to breakfast, which was being served in the sunroom. French toast casserole, bacon, sausage, scrambled eggs, granola and fresh fruit were the offerings. Carol chose some fruit and decided to try the French toast casserole as well.

Chatting with the inn's other guests over the delicious meal, Carol learned more about Stuart and the Treasure Coast, piquing her interest in the area. A couple of days ago, she wondered how she could possibly fill so many days, and now that her perspective had been changed, she wondered how she could possibly fit it all in to so few days.

After breakfast, Carol went back upstairs to plan her day. She decided to call Sarah to see how things were going at Enchantments.

"Hi, Sarah, it's Carol! How is everything going?"

"Carol, you've only been gone one day. Everything is just the same as it was on Wednesday evening when you left," Sarah said in a sarcastic tone. "You've got to learn to trust me and relax when you have the chance."

"I actually am learning, Sarah. I have a very good reason for calling. I have something I want to run by you. Don't be alarmed; I haven't made any decisions. I just want to make sure I keep you in the loop," Carol said. "Andrea beat me over the head with reality last night, and I've been re-evaluating my priorities. I plan to seriously consider the request Andrea and Jason put before me, and because of that, I need you and Tom to be aware that I might want to be bought out of the business. As I said, I haven't made any decisions, but I have promised to give it careful consideration."

Sarah was silent momentarily before she responded. "Naturally, I have mixed feelings about that. I don't think I'm ready to run this business on my own, and I know that I can't work with just anybody as a partner. However, that can all be worked out. I enjoy working with you and learning from you so much, and would hate for you to leave Oregon. On the other hand, it would be great for you and Andrea to live close to each other, especially with the baby on the way. Anyway, like I said, we can work all that out. Keep me updated about what you decide and enjoy yourself down there. I'll talk to Tom about the business."

"We can discuss details when the time comes," Carol said. "I haven't reached any decisions anyway, except to be more open-minded about the whole thing. I'm going shopping at some of the fun shops in downtown Stuart this morning, and this afternoon I am going with Andrea and Jason to see the house they are going to be making an offer on." Carol watched the boats on the St. Lucie River from her balcony as they talked. It was another beautiful sunny day, and she could imagine living in such a lovely area. "I should let you get back to work. Call me if you have any problems. I do have a great wireless connection here at the bed and breakfast, so you can email me if you need to as well."

"I'll call or email with any questions or problems," Sarah said. "However, I think I can handle most issues."

"I know you can. You learned from the best," Carol teased. She knew Sarah was completely capable. Sarah had always been a great employee, and if Carol didn't have total trust in her, she wouldn't have extended the invitation to her to be a partner.

"I sure did! Have a wonderful day, Carol. And if I don't talk to you before Sunday, have a Happy Mother's Day!"

Carol tossed her cell phone into her purse before leaving the inn. She had asked for directions to the shops she wanted to visit from David and Anna before breakfast. She walked toward Osceola Street, enjoying her leisurely stroll.

It had been far too long since she had taken the time to appreciate the moments of solitude like this. For years quiet time by herself had seemed like a sentence forced on her and she always tried to fill every waking moment with productivity. She had forgotten what a gift each minute of every day really was. She walked through the shops visiting with shop owners, buying several items, and then buying a huge tote bag in one of the shops so she could more easily carry her purchases.

Carol came out of Matilda's on Flagler Street when she thought she heard her name.

"Carol?" She turned to see Andrew Potter walking toward her. "I thought that was you," he said as he caught up to her. Indicating her bag, he continued, "It looks like you've been busy today."

She smiled at Andrew and said, "Yes, I've been trying to single-handedly support the community."

Andrew chuckled, "I'm on my way to grab some lunch at Osceola Street Café. Why don't you join me?"

Carol started to tell him she had things she planned to do this afternoon and couldn't eat lunch with him, and then thought better of it. "I'd like that, Andrew."

He was obviously pleased and a little surprised that she agreed to join him. "Can I carry your bag for you, Carol?" He asked and reached for her bag simultaneously.

She was used to doing everything herself, but uncharacteristically allowed him to take the part of gentleman. "Thank you, Andrew. It's nice to see that chivalry is still alive in the twenty-first century. These shops are lovely. I've had such a nice morning shopping and chatting with the store owners. I'm sure the tourists flock to this part of town, especially in the winter."

"Yes, I think some of these shops rely on tourists and snowbirds for a good percentage of their revenue," Andrew affirmed. "By the looks of your treasures, I think you've done your part to support the local retailers," he teased her. He slowed his steps. "This is the place, excellent food and great service," he said as he held the door for her.

They chose a table next to a window. Carol and Andrew talked easily over their lunch. They discussed their families and their jobs. Carol noticed Andrew talked about his sons, Brad and Drew, but didn't mention their mother. She almost asked but didn't want to give the impression that she was interested.

"Carol," Andrew interrupted her thoughts, "Andrea mentioned that you are a widow. I hope you don't feel I'm invading your privacy if I ask you about that?"

Andrew saw Carol's discomfort, and wished he hadn't said anything. "I'm sorry, Carol. I've overstepped my bounds."

"No, that's fine, Andrew. I guess I was just surprised for you to bring it up," Carol said. "My husband was killed in a car accident four years ago. The driver of the other car lost control, and hit my husband's car head-on. They think he died instantly. We would have celebrated our twenty-sixth anniversary a month later. In fact, Jim had planned a cruise for our anniversary." Carol paused briefly. She looked at Andrew, "Jim was my first real boyfriend. We dated for a couple of years in high school. When he graduated and left for college in Portland, we continued our relationship long distance. When he came home for Thanksgiving during my senior year, he proposed. Our wedding was only a few weeks after I graduated. I didn't know what to do when he died. I had never known life without him. My whole adult life up to that point had included Jim."

Andrew took Carol's hand, which was resting on top of the table, in his comfortingly.

"I'm sorry for your loss, Carol. I can't imagine how difficult it must have been for you."

Carol was touched, and looked at Andrew with moist eyes, "Thank you, Andrew. That means a lot to me. Most people are just uncomfortable, and say nothing when they hear about his death. After the first couple months, it seemed that people expected me to be done grieving and didn't want me to mention the fact that the man who had been in my life for more than a quarter of a century was gone. It means so much to have my loss acknowledged."

They shared a few minutes of silence. "What about you, Andrew? You haven't mentioned Brad and Drew's mother."

Andrew frowned, "We're divorced. We've been separated a little over a year, but the divorce was just finalized a couple of months ago. Molly is a recovering alcoholic. Because of that, most people think I'm the one who asked for the divorce. I tried to help her but I guess that wasn't what she needed. She went to AA and got help for her alcoholism on her own. I was so proud of her and gave as much support as I knew how. Just when I thought our lives could finally be normal, she told me she was having an affair and asked me for a divorce. We had been married almost thirty years, so I understand how you felt when you say you didn't know how to live without your husband."

"I'm sorry, Andrew. Now it's my turn to say that I can't imagine how difficult that was for you." Carol took Andrew's hand this time.

He patted her hand, "Thank you, Carol. It's actually fine now. We hadn't really been happy for a long time. I still wonder if a part of what had driven her to alcoholism was the fact that she was unhappy in our marriage. Molly and her new husband have moved back to New York, where he's from. So we have very little contact. Unlike your marriage, mine was a failure. I've learned I'm better off now. I had been in love with the girl I met in college and the woman I was married to wasn't that girl anymore. Fortunately for my sons, the façade that was our marriage didn't scar them. In fact, they apparently never realized Molly had a drinking problem. She hid that from them as well as we both managed to cover our unhappiness, even from ourselves. For Drew and Brad's sakes, I'm glad we were able to hold it together as long as we did." He looked at Carol, "That's enough of my babbling. I should get back to my office."

The waitress came by their table, "Can I get anything else for you?" She asked. Andrew had already paid the bill.

"No, thanks," Andrew answered. "We'll be going now." They both stood to leave.

"Thank you for lunch, Andrew. It was nice visiting with you," Carol said. They walked through the door back onto the street.

"The pleasure was all mine," he replied. "I usually eat my lunch alone, so this was indeed a treat. It was especially nice to have lunch with such an attractive lady across the table."

"Thank you, Andrew, you're such a charmer," Carol stated. She looked at her watch, "Oh, I'm going with Andrea and Jason to see the house they plan to buy...the one for which you prepared the insurance quote. They both love the house, so I'm not sure why they want my opinion."

Andrew chuckled, "Yes, when they talked to me about running the quote for them, I could tell they really wanted the house. I think they are more concerned with you liking the guest house. From what they told me, they are hoping you would want to live in the guest house while you look for a house. Are you still undecided about whether you are moving here?"

Carol nodded, "Yes, that's what they said they liked most about the guest house. I haven't made any decisions about moving here, but I am being more open to it. I do like the idea of being near my daughter, but I have a successful business that I would hate to walk away from."

Andrew stopped walking and said, "It might be easier to move when you have a successful business than if you had a struggling business. Selling a successful business is much easier than trying to unload a business not making any money. On the other hand, if you have a great manager, you can leave them in charge. Just some food for thought…"

Carol nodded thoughtfully, "That's all true. Well I better let you get back to your office. Andrea and Jason are picking me up soon, so I need to get back to the inn. Thanks again for lunch."

"Thank you for keeping me company," Andrew said. "I really enjoyed having lunch with you. We'll have to do it again if you have any free time before you go back to Oregon." They parted ways, walking in opposite directions; Carol headed toward the bed and breakfast, and Andrew walked back to his office, still thinking about Carol's emerald green eyes.

Carol, Andrea and Jason arrived at the house before the realtor, and walked around the property after getting out of the car.

"This is beautiful," Carol exclaimed. "I can see why you like it so much."

"Wait until you see the house," Jason said. "It's amazing. It's like it was built for us. It couldn't be more perfect for us if we had designed it ourselves." Andrea nodded in agreement.

They were chatting about the house when a Lincoln MKX pulled into the driveway. A tall man opened the door and stepped out of the vehicle. He looked to be about fifty, with dark blonde hair and a golden tan. He was wearing casual slacks and a palm tree print shirt.

"Sorry to keep you waiting. There was an accident on the turnpike and they re-routed us." He noticed Carol and extended his hand, "Hello there! I'm Steve...Steve Durkin."

Carol shook his hand, "Hi Steve, I'm Carol Davison, Andrea's mother."

Steve blinked several times, "No way you are old enough to be Andrea's mother. I could believe you are her older sister, but not her mother...unless you were eight when you had her."

"I was actually nine," Carol joked. "Thank you for the compliment, Steve."

Steve turned his attention to Jason and Andrea, "So what are you thinking, kids? You want me to write up an offer for you?" He asked as he unlocked the door.

Andrea answered, "We're almost positive we want to make the offer, Steve. We just want to look everything over again, and get Mom's opinion too. Did you talk to your client who might be interested in our condo?"

"Yes, I did and there is good news! He wants to buy it! I described it to him, and told him I sold it to you four years ago, sent him the pictures from when you bought it, and he wants to buy it for his winter home. He lives in Massachusetts, in Scituate, and has been coming down in the winter for the past few years. He said he's tired of renting when he comes down, so when I called him and told him about your place, he said he wants it," Steve said with enthusiasm.

"That's great," Jason said. "I can't believe how well that worked out."

The ladies had gone to the kitchen, and Andrea showed her mother around, pointing out her favorite features, and then moving on to the rest of the house, leaving Jason and Steve. Jason wanted to look at the garage again, so they went outside talking more about the Massachusetts gentleman interested in buying the condo.

When Steve walked into the garage, his interest was confirmed. It was big enough for their vehicle and his toys. Surprisingly, the structure was even insulated. They looked at the garage and were looking at the exterior of the house when Carol and Andrea walked up to them. "Steve, will you unlock the guest house?" Andrea asked. "I want to show it to my mom." She took hold of Jason's arm and looked up into his eyes. They shared a look of excitement and they both knew they had to make the offer today.

"Of course, I will," Steve said, reading their faces before walking toward the guest house. Steve's long legs moved him faster than the other three. He was unlocking the door when they walked up.

"Well, this is just darling," Carol said. "It's a little doll house!"

"There is a full kitchen with a large pantry, a full bedroom suite, a great room, and an office or whatever. A private patio on the side away from the main house is accessed by both the bedroom and the great room. It's just over 1,000 square feet. I have sold primary residence houses this size and smaller. I think when they built the place, they had a long term guest in mind," Steve explained as he stepped aside for them to walk through. "This place is a steal. They are trying to avoid foreclosure just like most of the rest of the country."

Carol looked through the house in silence. The kitchen was definitely big enough for her, even if she was entertaining company. She was amazed at the bedroom suite, with a fabulous walk in closet, and the bathroom had a shower and a big garden tub. She opened the French doors leading to the patio, and imagined sitting with her morning coffee and watching birds flying over the Intracoastal.

Andrea walked out and stood near her mother in silence, Jason a few steps behind her. Carol looked at Andrea and smiled, "The house I lived in with my mother was about this size. It's remarkable that they have built such an exceptional guest house. I have to say, I imagined a much smaller place." Carol moved closer to Andrea and put her arm around her waist, kissing her on the cheek. "I think you two have definitely found a treasure in this place." She looked over to Jason and smiled, including him in the conversation. "You'd be foolish not to buy at this price, and I'm still not making any commitments yet, but if I do move here, this guest house would definitely suit my needs until I find my own place. Just be aware that if I get too comfortable, I might stay," she said with a wink.

Andrea hugged her mother, and then rushed over to hug and kiss Jason. "Let's ask Steve to write up the offer now!" She ran over to the door and shouted, "Steve!"

Steve appeared in the doorway, "Yes?" He looked from Andrea to Jason and back, "Do you have any questions?"

"Yes, we do. How quick can you write up the offer?" Jason asked.

Steve smiled, "I had a feeling you would ask me that. I have it ready except for the particulars. We can finish it up here, if you want. I'll just get my briefcase and we can sit here in the kitchen if you want."

♥

They went for a casual dinner after writing up the offer. Carol had insisted on buying them dinner to celebrate. They went to Key Lime Tiki Bar. It was a warm evening and they sat leisurely enjoying the night.

"Steve said we could hear back on the offer by tomorrow," Jason said. "He also said he will talk to the gentleman from Scituate about writing up an offer."

Jason's phone started to vibrate, and he reached in his pocket to pull it out, "I wonder if this could be Steve already." He looked at his phone, nodded, and stood up to walk out to the street.

"Oh, Mom, I'm so excited. Do you think Steve could possibly have heard back on the offer already? It's only been two hours."

"It could be that he's heard back on the offer. He did say the sellers are trying to avoid foreclosure," Carol said. She smiled at her daughter, "You remind me of when you were a little girl when you get excited."

Jason came back to the table and sat down. He took Andrea's hand in his and grinned broadly, "They accepted the offer. There is no counter-offer. In 30 days, the house is ours!"

Andrea squealed with excitement, and wrapped her arms around her husband's neck.

Chapter Nine

Mother's Day morning was beautiful, with no clouds in the sky and the sun warming the earth to a comfortable temperature. The azure sky was a lovely backdrop to the teal colored ocean. The gentle breeze acting as a ceiling fan sent by God, pushing the moist air just enough to keep it from becoming heavy.

"What a nice sermon! I can see the appeal this church and the pastor hold for you. This seems like such an upbeat church," Carol exclaimed. "A nice way to spend a Sunday morning. He really made the mothers in church feel special."

"You *are* special. Happy Mother's Day, Mom," Andrea said, giving her mother a hug. "I hope you're ready to go out on the boat – and I hope you're hungry. We have a nice brunch packed."

"I'm starving, and I'm ready to work on my tan," Carol said with a smile. She wore a lovely yellow strapless sundress that she had purchased on Friday morning, with a white cardigan over it to be appropriate for church.

"Jason! Andrea!" They heard someone shout from behind them. They all turned and Steve, their realtor, caught up to them. "I don't want to interrupt your day, but I saw you in church so I thought I would go ahead and tell you what I found out regarding your condo. I talked to George Popovich, from Massachusetts. I thought we could negotiate verbally and get an agreement before writing up the deal. Sometimes it works better that way when one or both parties are out of the area. Unfortunately, Mr. Popovich is coming in pretty low. It might be best if we have another agent represent him, so that I can give you the best representation. I'll leave that up to you and him. If you don't mind, I'll just go over the figures he is talking about real quick. You can talk about it today, and then let me know tomorrow or the next day what you want me to do."

Andrea and Jason looked at each other, and Jason said, "That sounds fine. How low is he?"

They sat on a bench outside the church and went over the offer, discussed some of their options, and agreed they would let Steve know their decision the following morning.

"Sorry to interrupt your morning. Happy Mother's Day, Carol…and to you as well, Andrea," Steve said acknowledging her impending motherhood before he turned to walk quickly away.

"That man is a bundle of energy, isn't he?" Carol asked, not expecting an answer. She started walking toward the car. Andrea and Jason followed her quietly. The mood had changed, Andrea was obviously disappointed and Jason was doing his best to cover his frustration. Carol changed the subject to try to lighten the mood.

"So what is this delicious brunch that you packed?" She asked.

"Well, you'll just have to wait and see," Jason teased. "If we tell you before we have you captive on the boat, you might decide not to spend the day with us."

"Jason, that's not true," Andrea retorted. She slugged his shoulder playfully. He turned and started tickling her. She giggled and lightheartedly said, “Stop! Stop that now, young man. You’ll make me wet my pants!” All three were laughing as they reached the car.

♥

Jason carried the picnic basket and cooler to the boat as the ladies boarded. It was a perfect day to enjoy a relaxing ride on the Intracoastal. As Jason was navigating away from the dock, he turned his head to talk to Carol, “Andrea told me all about your shopping trip yesterday. It sounds like you both had a great time!”

“We did!” Carol agreed. “It’s been a long time since we have been able to spend the day shopping together. I’m sure she told you all about the baby furniture we picked out.”

Andrea started to unpack the brunch fare. “Mom, would you like a glass of champagne? I’m having sparkling cider, but I brought champagne for you and Jason.”

Jason popped the cork and poured two glasses of champagne. “Here’s to two of my favorite mothers.” They clinked glasses and sipped their champagne and cider.

“Jason, speaking of favorite mothers, what is your mother doing today?” Carol asked.

“We invited her to come with us, but my sister beat us to the punch. She and her husband invited Mom and Dad to visit them in Orlando this weekend. They’re having a Sea World Mother’s Day,” Jason responded. “Janet’s kids are three and five years now, and they wanted Grandma to go to

Disney, but Janet suggested they compromise and do Sea World."

Carol laughed, "Well either way, I'm sure your mom is just happy to be with her grandchildren."

Andrea finished unpacking the food and suggested they dish up their plates, "I made a quiche, and we have bagels and cream cheese, strawberries, kiwi and melons."

They enjoyed the brunch. The boat ride was relaxing; it could have been considered boring by some, but the company was excellent and they all had a wonderful day. They all had a wonderful day, that is, until the subject of the buying the house and selling the condo came up.

Andrea's mood changed instantly and dramatically as soon as they started talking about real estate. "We'll just have to forget about buying the house. If Mr. Poppadoppa, or whatever his name is, wants to buy our condo for such a low price, how can we possibly sell it? And if we can't sell the condo, we shouldn't buy the house. It's just irresponsible to take on two mortgages!" She was nearly in tears.

Jason put his arm around her to comfort her, "Sweetheart, if Mr. Popovich doesn't want to buy the condo at a reasonable price, we'll just have to find another buyer. And if we don't find one, then the house wasn't meant to be. We have each other, and we have our baby. Family is what is important, not a building. Yes, we both love that house, but it's really just a pile of sticks and stones. Let's just pray about it. O.K?" He had both arms wrapped around her now.

Andrea sniffed, and hugged her husband. She looked up into his eyes, "O.K. You're right. All I really want is to have my husband and my baby, and hopefully my mother, close to me."

Carol sat staring out over the water deep in thought, trying to give them a moment of privacy; at least as much privacy as they could have while on the boat. "Well, do you want my view on this?"

She startled the couple. They had almost forgotten where they were.

"Of course," Jason and Andrea both said at once.

"Jinx!" They said in unison, and laughed. Carol joined in the laughter and they momentarily forgot about the conversation they'd been having. Carol was amazed at how quickly Andrea's moods changed.

Jason was the first to compose himself. "What's your sage advice, Carol?"

She looked at Jason and Andrea for a moment before she spoke. "You're getting an excellent deal on the house you're buying. Counter the offer from Mr. Popovich, but not too high. If you have to go lower than you wanted, realize that it's a tough market, and you don't want to lose out on the new house because you can't get exactly what you want for the condo. Jason's right, the house is really a pile of sticks and stones, but while we're here on earth, we all have to live somewhere. You might as well live somewhere you love if you can." They were both listening to Carol's opinion and nodded. "Life is all about compromises; sometimes you have to give a little more than you want, and sometimes you get a little more than you give. It's up to you to decide how much you're willing to give to get what you want." She looked away, thinking she might need to take some of her own advice. The wisdom she was imparting on them could also be applied to her decision about whether or not she should move to Florida. She looked back to them. "That's my opinion, for what it's worth...about two cents actually," she joked.

Jason and Andrea looked at each other, and without saying a word, they both hugged Carol tightly.

♥

The young couple followed Carol's advice, and asked Steve to counter the offer on Monday. They ended up accepting less than they wanted, but at least it was closer and they wouldn't miss out on their dream house. For the rest of the week, Andrea and Jason showed Carol around Stuart and other parts of the Treasure Coast after work. Carol explored the area on her own accord during the day.

On Friday, Carol decided to have a lazy day. She had purchased a new swimsuit, a brown tankini with leopard trim and a matching wrap. Anna and Brian loaned her a beach chair and umbrella. She stepped into her new leopard print flip flops, grabbed her new leopard sunglasses, and poking Claire Cook's book, *Life's a Beach*, into her tote bag along with a beach towel, sun screen and a bottle of water, she headed out.

Carol put the top down on her rented mustang, and drove across the Intracoastal to Hutchinson Island, feeling younger than she had in years. She pulled into the parking lot at Stuart Beach, and was surprised to find very few cars there. She chose a nice spot on the beach and set up the beach chair and umbrella and kicked off her flip flops before walking down to test the water temperature. She was pleasantly surprised at how warm it was, and before she knew it she ran back up to her chair to deposit her wrap. She was suddenly self conscious about being in public wearing only a swim suit, but quickly put aside those feelings, dove into the ocean and swam along the coastline. Using muscles she had barely used in years, Carol tired quickly and walked back to her beach chair feeling exhilarated. She picked up her towel and dried off, watching the ocean waves. Wrapping her cover up around her waist, Carol thought how she had missed coming to the beach. She and Jim used to go to the beach in Oregon often, and she had always felt at peace listening to the sounds of the ocean and was often mesmerized watching the waves. After Jim died, she never went back to enjoy her favorite refuge.

She sat in the beach chair watching the waves and soaking up the sun, thinking about how much she had missed because she missed her husband and didn't want to enjoy life if he couldn't. She understood now that she shouldn't stop living, but live for both of them. The fact that Jim was no longer here to enjoy life's great pleasures didn't mean that she shouldn't either, but rather realize how important it is to appreciate what life has to offer.

Carol closed her eyes and tipped her head back, taking in the warmth from the sun and listening to the ocean's waves. She sat like that for a while, and felt more at peace than she had in years.

The sound of children's laughter caused Carol open her eyes and look toward the children. Two young women and three children had just arrived at the beach and the ladies were scoping out the perfect spot as the children ran to the water. Carol watched the children for a few minutes, imagining coming to the beach with her grandchild, or hopefully grandchildren. Her recognition of what she needed to do had been confirmed repeatedly in the past week.

Carol would be leaving on Monday to fly back to Portland. She decided to wait until Sunday to talk to Andrea and Jason about her decision. There would be a lot of details to figure out in regards to her home and business, but at least she wouldn't need to worry about a place to live in Stuart.

Feeling better about life than she had since she lost Jim, Carol wondered why it had taken her so long to come to the ocean. The beach, the ocean, the waves had always been her solace. She smiled, and knew Jim would be pleased with her. "I finally got it, Jim," she said aloud, looking up to the sky.

She sat watching the waves and the children for a few more minutes before picking up her book to read.

♥

Carol's water bottle was empty and she figured she had spent enough time in the sun. She didn't want to get sunburned and look like a tourist. Packing up her towel, book, and beach gear, she felt good about the decisions she had reached during her stay in Florida.

Squeals of laughter drew her attention back to the children playing. They were making sand castles and laughing when the waves erased their efforts. It was sort of nature's Etch-a-Sketch. These children were making memories that would last a lifetime. They might forget events that seem more significant, but they would remember spending time at the beach with family and friends, playing in the sand and the ocean.

Carol saw a man jogging along the water's edge and thought that's what she should have been doing instead of lounging. She wasn't fat, but she certainly didn't burn calories as fast as she used to, and could stand to take off a little weight. Carol turned and walked toward the ramp that would take her to the parking lot. She had just reached the ramp when she heard her name. "Carol, I'm glad I ran into you," Andrew was the man she had seen jogging.

"Literally, it seems," Carol laughed. She noticed Andrew's fit physique, and hoped he neither sensed her appreciation of his fitness nor noted the few extra pounds she was packing. She suddenly felt uncomfortable, as if she was in junior high school talking to the cute boy while she had zits and greasy hair. What was wrong with her?

"Yes, well I normally jog early in the morning, but I took the day off and slept in. That felt good, except it made me lazy. After reading a book on my deck most of the morning, I decided I better get a run in. I'm a stickler about my exercise. I turned fifty this year, on Valentines Day actually. I woke up that morning and realized I was out of shape. I gave myself a birthday gift of finding the toughest personal trainer around. My dad had a heart attack and died when he was fifty-one, he was overweight and I just didn't want to follow in his path." Andrew realized that he didn't need to share so much, "Sorry to bore you with my health report," he grinned.

Carol smiled, "Don't be silly, you didn't bore me. You couldn't have been that out of shape to be this fit in only a couple of months." She readjusted her load as the umbrella had started to slip.

"Oh, I'm sorry. I've been rude. You've been standing there with an armload as I have been prattling on," Andrew said as he reached out to help her. "Let me carry some of that for you." He grabbed the beach umbrella and chair, and they both turned to walk toward the parking lot.

"Thank you, Andrew, but it was really not that much stuff. You didn't need to help me," Carol said.

"I have a great idea," Andrew said, ignoring her comment. "If you're not busy, there is a great place to eat in Jupiter. I have a change of clothes in my car, and it'll take me ten minutes to shower, and we can go down to Jupiter for lunch. Want to?"

"I don't know, Andrew. How far away do you have to go for a shower?" They had reached Carol's rental car and she popped the trunk.

"About fifty feet," Andrew answered, putting Carol's beach gear in the trunk for her.

"They have showers here. It will literally take me about ten minutes. How about it, Carol? Will you to come to Jupiter with me for lunch?"

"Well, I really didn't have any plans, but I'm only wearing a swimsuit and cover up. I can't go to a restaurant dressed like this."

"Might I remind you that this is Florida…"

"It very well may be. But *I* don't go to restaurants dressed this way."

"Why don't you go to the inn and change, and I'll be right behind you after I shower. I'll pick you up," he looked at his watch, "in 30 minutes. You'll be glad you did because lunch, or breakfast or dinner for that matter, at Guanabanas is an experience you should not miss." Andrew looked at Carol with puppy dog eyes. "Please…"

Carol laughed, "You're incorrigible! I suppose I can't say no. Fine, I'll see you in half an hour." Without another word, or even a glance back, she got in the car and drove away.

♥

It seemed like it only took a couple of minutes to drive to Jupiter. Once again, Carol and Andrew fell into easy conversation like old friends and they reached the restaurant quickly. They got out of Andrew's car and the valet parked it as they turned to Guanabanas.

"Wow!" Was all Carol could say as they walked up to the doorway. It was an outdoor restaurant with tropical décor; palm trees, a lovely pond with waterfalls, a rock pathway, a creek with rock bridges, tiki torches. "It feels like we're on a tropical island. This is wonderful!"

"I'd like to bring you here for dinner sometime. I know you're going back to Oregon soon, but if you have any time before you go, maybe you'll let me buy you dinner. See the stage over there? With the palm roof? They have live music here on the weekends."

The hostess walked up to them, "Two for lunch?" She asked.

"Yes," Andrew responded. "Could we get a table on the river?"

The hostess smiled and replied, "Yes, we have a couple of river tables open." She led them to their table and gave them menus.

They both started looking at their menus, but Andrew already knew what he wanted to order and set his menu aside. Carol glanced at him, "Getting back to what you were saying, Andrew, I appreciate the offer of dinner, but I'm leaving Monday and I don't have a free evening before then." She looked back down at her menu.

"I'm sorry to hear that. Have you made a decision about moving here?"

The waitress came for their orders just then. "I'll have the Avocado Bacon Mango Salad," Carol said.

"Nice choice," the waitress commented, before turning to Andrew. "And what can I get for you, sir?"

"I have to have the Fat Cuban," Andrew responded. After the waitress walked away, he looked at Carol and explained, "The Fat Cuban is the best pork sandwich. So anyway, I had just asked you about whether you've made a decision about moving to Florida."

Carol nodded as though she had forgotten he had asked. "I don't know yet. It's a tough decision. It is lovely here, and I have really enjoyed spending time with my daughter, but I just don't know yet." Since she hadn't given Andrea her decision, she didn't feel that it would be right to tell anyone else.

The waitress came with their drinks, and Carol took the opportunity to sip her strawberry Margarita, and changed the subject, "Mmm, this is delicious! Do you come to Guanabanas often, Andrew?"

He got the message that she didn't want to talk about moving. "Not as much as I'd like, but enough to know that I like to eat a Fat Cuban for lunch," he smiled. Carol smiled back. They enjoyed their lunch and talked about safe subjects for the rest of the meal.

When the waitress came by and asked if they had room for dessert, Andrew said, "You haven't had coconut cream pie until you eaten it here. Share a piece with me, Carol?" His smile convinced her to try it.

When they got up to leave Carol said, "You were right, Andrew. That was the best coconut cream pie I've ever had. I'm sorry I won't have time before I leave to come back here for dinner with you. It's a lovely restaurant and I would have enjoyed coming back here with you."

They chatted comfortably on the drive back to Stuart. When they arrived at Treasure Coast Paradise Inn, Andrew hurried around to the passenger side to open the door for Carol as he always did. "Carol, I'm glad I met you and was able to spend some time with you. I would really like to see you again. I hope you do move to Florida." He leaned in to kiss her, and she turned her head.

"Please don't," was all she said.

"I'm sorry. I don't know why I did that…except for the fact that I'm very attracted to you and I like being with you. I really enjoy your company." He looked at her apologetically.

Carol smiled, "I enjoy your company too, Andrew. I'm just not ready for that."

"I'll be going now. Can I see you again before you leave?"

"I'll be pretty tied up with Andrea. She and Jason have your number. If I get some time, I'll call you." She turned and walked up the steps to the inn, leaving Andrew to watch her walk away.

Chapter Ten

It was hard to believe it was already Sunday. Carol's time in Florida had gone by quickly, especially the last two days. While Carol was eager to go home and start the preparations to move to Florida, she was also sad that her trip was drawing to an end.

It would be with a heavy-heart that she would leave Joan, who had been such a dear friend and neighbor for many years, but she knew Joan already supported her decision. It was with a plethora of emotions that she would be making these changes in her life. She had enjoyed the time with her daughter; something that she hadn't truly recognized the value of in several years.

After church that morning, Carol asked Andrea and Jason to take a walk with her on the beach. "Since I'm leaving in the morning, I would love to spend some time with the two of you walking on the beach."

They agreed, and all chatted happily on the drive to Stuart Beach. It was a beautiful morning and as they reached the parking lot, they found only one other car parked there. The three of them walked down to the water's edge talking about nothing in particular.

When a lull in the conversation came, Carol suddenly stopped and looked at her daughter and son-in-law. "I told you about spending the morning on the beach the other day. It was a wonderful morning. I watched some children playing and I thought about how they were making memories that would be far more special than events that would seem more important." She paused looking out at the waves, while Andrea and Jason watched her expectantly.

Carol was silent as she chose her words, not quite sure about all she intended to say. She held Andrea's hand and said, "We shared some fun times during my stay here and created some memories I will cherish forever. You respected my wish not to talk to me about moving, and I appreciate that." She paused again.

Andrea started to say something and Carol said, "Please let me finish." She started walking again and they followed suit. "When I was watching those children, I couldn't help but reminisce about all the times we had gone to Seaside or Cannon Beach when you were little. Then I thought about what is really important in life. I realized that what is important in my life is you," she said looking into Andrea's eyes. "You and Jason are the most important part of my life."

Andrea had tears in her eyes yet again. Carol stopped walking again and looked at Jason before taking both his and Andrea's hands in hers. "I want to be a part of your lives, and I want to be around to see your baby grow. I don't want to be a long distance grandmother. I have decided that I will move to Florida." Andrea squealed with excitement and threw her arms around her mother.

Carol hugged Andrea before continuing, "I have a lot to figure out with the house and the business. I already told Sarah to be prepared for this decision, so I will sit down with her and Tom when I get back and see what we can figure out for Enchantments. The hardest thing for me will be the house. But as you reminded us, Jason, a house is just a pile of sticks and stones. It's difficult for me to think of my home as a pile of sticks and stones, but that is what it is. When Joan dropped me off at the Portland airport she said to me that my memories with Jim aren't in that house; they're stored in my head; they're in my head as well as my heart. I just need to keep telling myself that because I *do* want to be down here with you."

"Oh, Momma, I'm so happy," Andrea exclaimed. She hugged her mother again. Jason joined them in the hug.

"Looks like a Kodak moment!"

They all turned.

"Andrew, what a surprise," Jason exclaimed.

Andrew chuckled, "I like to jog on the beach. I try to get out here four or five days a week."

Andrea grabbed Andrews arm, "Guess what, Andrew? My mom has decided to move to Florida! I'm so excited I could scream!"

Andrew smiled and was obviously pleased. He looked at Carol, "Well, that is good news!" He gave Andrea a quick hug. "Hey, what are you three doing this afternoon? Brad and Angie are coming over to my place and we're going to throw some burgers on the grill. You should join us. I have plenty of food."

Carol shook her head, "No, I'm sorry, Andrew, but we just don't have time. You see I'm leaving in the morning."

"What do you mean we don't have time, Mom? We have to eat anyway. Andrew, of course we can come over for your barbecue," Andrea said.

"I suppose you're right, Andrea," Carol agreed hesitantly. "What can we bring, Andrew?"

"Don't bring a thing! I have everything for the burgers. I also have chips, melons, and plenty of beverages. Brad and Angie are bringing salad of some sort, and Angie makes a great Dr. Pepper cake."

"A what?" Carol asked, astounded by such a preposterous sounding cake.

"It's a southern thing, Carol," Jason said. "You'll love it."

♥

They had all finished eating and were enjoying a cocktail on the deck, except Andrea, who was having iced tea. "Angie, the cake was delicious," Carol said. "I never would have thought Dr. Pepper in a cake would be good, but it really is. I hope you'll share the recipe with me."

"Of course I will, Carol," Angie replied, putting her hand on Carol's forearm. "I'll email it to you. So you're moving to Florida. I'm so glad; I know how much Andrea has been hoping for this. You'll love living here. I am from Michigan and I don't miss winters at all."

Carol smiled, "Well, winters aren't too bad in Portland. They're not like the winters where I grew up in Spokane, Washington. But it will be nice not to worry about slick roads. The main thing is that I've missed my daughter for all these years."

Carol leaned over and kissed Andrea's cheek. She looked at her watch. It was nearly eight. "I should probably get back to the inn soon. My flight leaves West Palm at a quarter to six tomorrow morning, and I haven't even packed."

"You're right, Mom. But I'm going to miss you so much," Andrea said, tears forming in her eyes. Jason put his arm around her.

"I'll be back before you know it," Carol said, and hugged her daughter.

Andrew stood up and extended his right hand, "Carol, it's been a pleasure meeting you." Carol reached to shake his hand, but he brought her hand up and kissed it softly. "I hope I will be able to get to know you better when you come back."

Chapter Eleven

Carol walked into her house Monday afternoon feeling tired and energized at the same time. Joan had picked her up at the airport and they stopped for lunch before driving to Carol's house. Carol had wanted to come straight home and unpack her bags, but Joan had insisted on buying her lunch so they could sit and relax while they caught up. Joan had been thrilled at learning Carol's news.

Joan helped Carol bring her bags in from the car, "I put all your mail over here on the kitchen counter. That yellow rose bush by your kitchen door was looking poorly so I trimmed it back a little and gave it some love. It looks better now. Do you want some help unpacking or anything, sweetie?"

"No, but thank you, Joan. It won't take me long to unpack and start my laundry. But you're welcome to stick around and keep me company. I'll make some tea," Carol said, walking over to get the tea kettle.

Joan said, "I'll make the tea, Carol. Go ahead and get your laundry going."

Carol smiled and hugged Joan, "Thank you, Joan. I'm really going to miss you when I move to Florida. You're such a big part of my life. You've always been here for me."

Joan gave Carol's arm a loving squeeze, "You've always been here for me as well, my dear. You're like a daughter to me. The great thing about you moving to Florida is that now I have a place to get away from the gray and dreary January days."

♥

Tuesday evening, Carol met with Sarah and Tom to discuss the business arrangements. It was agreed that Carol would remain as an advising partner for at least the first year, at which time they would reevaluate the arrangement. Rebecca, the gal they had hired as an assistant in April was doing a great job, which would make it easier for Sarah to take on managing the business. Sarah was more than capable of handling the day to day business operations.

Carol hadn't planned on going back to Enchantments until Wednesday, as she had decided to take Tuesday morning to sleep off her jet lag. When she did get up that morning she sat in her favorite chair with her coffee to map out her game plan for the tasks before her. Even though Tom was a commercial real estate broker he did handle some residential properties, so when Carol was ready to list the house, it had been agreed that Tom would do that for her.

She knew that the first thing she needed to do was to go through her home and sort through everything, eliminating anything that wasn't important enough to move 3,000 miles. She felt that the most difficult part of this particular task would be going through the things of Jim's that she still had. After he died, many of his items had been boxed up and left in his office. Carol rarely went in there. She decided she would ask Joan to help her with this, which was a big step for her as she wasn't in the habit of asking for help.

"Why don't I go through the room without you, Carol? Anything I find that I'm not sure about, I will separate for you to look at. That way you don't have to look through all of it. Obviously, if you haven't looked at it in four years, there isn't too much in there that you really need," Joan said to Carol. "You know that I'll be careful not to get rid of anything important."

Carol hesitated, but knew Joan was right. She had been holding on for all these years to the things in Jim's office. "I guess I just always felt that if I got rid of any of Jim's things, I was throwing away a part of him. I couldn't bring myself to do that. It felt disloyal." Joan waited as Carol obviously had more to say. "I still wear one of his Oregon Ducks sweatshirts to bed. He's not here to keep me warm, so I snuggle up in his sweatshirt." Carol had tears in her eyes.

Joan walked across the room and hugged Carol. "I had no idea you did that, sweetie. You keep that sweatshirt because it gives you comfort, but letting go of Jim's things is not letting go of Jim. They are just things. I am willing to bet there are just a handful of items in Jim's office that you need to keep. So let's get to work. I'll start going through his office, and you can work on the rest of the house."

When all was said and done, Joan only had a small cardboard box for Carol to go through. It was mostly paperwork; financial statements and such. There was also a box of photographs that she knew Carol would want to keep. They had been at it all afternoon, and it was nearly seven. Neither of them had eaten and they decided to send out for Chinese food.

The food arrived and they took it out to the patio to eat. It was a lovely evening in late May, but Carol couldn't help but think about how much warmer it would be to eat on the patio in Florida. They were both tired; it was that good kind of tired, where they had a great sense of accomplishment and satisfaction.

"Carol, I found something today that you should read," Joan said as they finished dinner. "I wanted to wait until we had eaten. I don't know if I should stay or go while you read it."

"What is it, Joan?"

Joan paused for a moment before telling her, "It's a letter from Jim to you."

Carol gasped and drew her hands to her heart. "Did you read it?"

Joan shook her head, "No, dear. It's in an envelope with your name on it. The envelope is sealed."

"Read it to me…no, I'll read it later when I go to bed…no, stay with me and I'll read it now," Carol vacillated before finally holding out her hand. "O.K. Go ahead and give it to me. I'll read it now. Please stay with me." She picked up her wine glass and sipped before opening the envelope. She looked at Joan, possibly for strength, and removed the letter from the envelope.

My Darling Carol,

I've been sitting in my office working this evening while you're shooting a wedding. I've been thinking about life - our lives in particular. I just booked a cruise to celebrate our 25th wedding anniversary. We've dreamed and talked about doing it for years and I decided it was past time for us to do it. I feel that we need to focus on us a little more than we have been. We both work too much. You are my life. You are my reason for living. I love you so much and I thought about how I would not want to live without you in my life.

If you're reading this, it means that something has happened to me, that you are forced to live your life without me in yours, and that you have had to clean out my office. I pray you never see this letter and that we can grow old together. If you are reading this, there's no way I can know what happened, I only want to say that I'm sorry. For whatever reason I am not there for you, I'm sorry I'm not there to share the rest of your life with you. Please forgive me.

I fell for you when I first saw you in the hall at Rogers High School. I know it's cliché, but you really are my soul mate. I am the luckiest man in the world that I have been able to share my life with you.

The main reason I wanted to write this letter is that I was thinking about what I would wish for you if I can't be there with you.

Carol, I hope you know after all these years we have shared together, that what I want most for you is your happiness. If something should happen to take me away from you, I still mostly just want you to be happy. Live for both of us. Do things we never did together. Do things we did together and loved doing. Get everything out of life that you can.

I hope for you to live close to Andrea. If I'm not there, my hope is that you move to be near her, or she moves to be near you. We only have one child and it has been harder than we ever imagined for both of us that she lives so far away. If I'm not here, make sure you have each other!

My love, this is important...don't be alone. If I am not there to make you happy, find a man who will. Don't find him the next day, but don't be lonely either. If I can't be the man to make you happy, find another man who can. It would make me a happy man to know you are always happy. I don't like to think of you with another man, but more than that I don't like to think of you alone. Find someone I would like to have as a friend, and someone who will romance you and grow old with you.

I love you so much, Carol. You are my world. I want to be your world, and just remember that my wish is for your world to be wonderful. I have always tried to make that happen. If I can't be there to do it, the only thing I ask is that you make it happen.

All my Love,
Jim

When Carol finished reading the letter, she held it to her chest silently for several minutes, a single tear running down her cheek. Her eyes were moist and another tear spilled out, "I miss him so much, Joan," she said to her friend. "I want you to read this too." Carol handed the letter to Joan.

Joan took the letter to read it. Carol sat back in her chair with her glass of wine and thought about what Jim had written. She sat patiently as Joan read the letter. Joan glanced at Carol a few times as she read.

"Well, my dear," Joan started as she handed the letter back to Carol and patted her friend's hand, "I believe you are making Jim happy. You have come to the right decision for you, and also the one that would please Jim."

Chapter Twelve

When Joan went home, Carol went inside and was still thinking about the letter. She called Andrea.

"Andrea, I had to call you. I've started going through things to figure out what is coming with me to Florida. Joan offered to help, and she worked all afternoon on Jim's office. She found a letter that your dad had written to me. I want to read it to you." Carol read the letter to Andrea, who was immediately in tears. Carol could hear Andrea crying, "Are you ok, sweetie?"

"Yes, I'm fine, Mom. It's just that I never thought about how difficult it must have been for both of you when I moved to Florida, but I have always felt bad about the years I missed not knowing that Dad would die so young. I never would have moved to Florida when I did if I would have had any idea that I would lose my father too soon. But I'm so happy that you are moving here. Thank you for reading that to me, Mom."

Carol said, "I knew it was important for you to hear it, Andrea. Don't feel badly about moving away when you did, sweetie. Your best friend was going to college down there so you wanted to join her. That's natural. Your daddy understood that. We both did. We just really missed you. None of us could have known we would lose him so soon. If I've learned anything these past few months it's that we can't do anything to change the past, but we can take the lessons we've learned from it to make our futures better. We cherish our old memories as we build new ones."

"That's true, Mom. Are you doing ok after reading this letter?"

"Yes, I am. I miss your father terribly...and it made me feel strange that he had thought about this so intensely so close to when the accident happened. The fact that he wrote this the same night he booked our cruise really saddens me, especially since we never got to take that trip, and it was something we always wanted to do. After reading the letter, I realized that one of my priorities needs to be making sure that I take a Caribbean cruise sometime soon. Jim would want me to do that. We had always dreamed of going on a cruise, and we missed out on the cruise that he planned for us. When I read the part where he wrote that I should do things we had never done together, I immediately thought of that cruise. "

"You're right, Mom! You should make plans for that. Maybe you can take the cruise with Joan."

"That's a great idea! I'm sure she'd love it."

Before they ended the call Andrea said, "I was going to call you first thing tomorrow morning, but since I have you on the phone, there's something I want ask you," Andrea said. "We decided to find out the sex of the baby and we chose a name. Do you want to know?"

"Of course I do."

"Jamie Grace – Jamie is for Daddy, and Grace is Jason's grandmother. We're having a baby girl!"

It was Carol's turn to cry, "Andrea, you've made me so happy. You couldn't have picked a better name for my granddaughter. Your father would be so proud!"

♥

The rest of the week went by quickly and Carol's focus was on the business. She went over things with Sarah in between helping customers and other business matters. After much discussion, it was decided that Carol would gradually take less of an active role in order to help Sarah become more accustomed to running the business. This would also enable Carol to take care of personal matters. Since Carol hadn't taken a salary from the business in years, that wasn't an issue. Between the proceeds of selling Jim's business and the huge life insurance policy Jim had, Carol lived comfortably.

Carol went through all the appointments on the books and decided which of them were important for her to do. She realized she had to be there to do the wedding photos for Monica's wedding in September. "I dread telling Andrea this," she said aloud more to herself, but Sarah heard.

"What dreadful thing do you need to tell Andrea?" Sarah asked, chuckling at her wording.

Carol looked up and smiled at Sarah. "I really should be here to do Monica and David's wedding in September. I know Andy was hoping I would be able to move before that. She wanted me to be there to share her last trimester."

"Carol, you can always move down there, and come back up for that wedding," Sarah stated matter-of-factly. "I know Monica had her heart set on you doing her wedding photos, and Andrea wouldn't have a problem with you leaving for a few days, or even a week, so you can come back up to do a wedding."

"Now, see there, that's why you're going to do great without me. You're thinking like a manager already, and I am already not thinking like anything," Carol joked.

♥

On Saturday morning, Carol decided that since she was making changes in her life, it was time for her to start exercising again. She dressed in a navy blue Nike jogging suit, and laced her Nike running shoes that had been lost in the back of her closet. She knew that since it had been a few years since she had gone jogging, she wouldn't get far today. She felt that it was important to start somewhere, and today was the day.

She lived just a few blocks from a middle school, so she would walk to the school track, run four laps and walk home. That was her plan anyway, and she would see just how out of shape she was after she started.

The morning was a little chilly, but that would probably turn out to be a good thing because once Carol started on the track, she would warm up quickly. She was suddenly thinking of Andrew jogging on the beach and just as quickly tried to brush that image from her mind. What in the world had made her think about him all of a sudden? She didn't know, but she would do her best not to let that happen again. Her heart rate rose quickly and she was breathing heavily, but it was easier to jog the mile than she had thought it would be. She didn't seem to be in as bad of shape as she thought; tomorrow morning might tell a different story once she found out which muscles would be screaming at her.

Walking back home from the track, Carol felt exhilarated and wondered why it had taken her so long to start jogging again. Of course, that is assuming she would stay on track and be diligent about exercise.

Once she was home, Carol started the coffee brewing before taking her shower. Dressing in her most comfortable pair of jeans and an old sweatshirt, thin from years of wear, she poured her coffee and started working on the guest room. Her thoughts went to her visit to Florida in May. For some reason she remembered how she had snapped at Andrew when she first met him. Jason had made a comment about her house and business being replaceable, but her family wasn't. When Andrew agreed with Jason, Carol had told him it wasn't any of his business. Again, Carol forced Andrew from her thoughts. She focused on her task at hand. Since there were relatively few items in this room it seemed the best place to start, and she would work room by room until she had the house done.

The phone rang and Carol picked up the cordless phone and her empty coffee cup, answering the phone as she walked to the kitchen for a refill.

The caller was Carol's sister-in-law, Jim's sister, Nancy.

"Nancy, what a nice surprise! I'm so glad to hear from you. How are you?"

"I'm doing well, Carol. And you?"

"I'm the best I've been in a long time. Thank you for asking. What's up?"

"I'm calling to ask a favor. Roger has been offered a transfer back to Portland, and I was calling to see if we could stay with you from time to time as we need to start house hunting. Feel free to tell me no. We can obviously stay in a hotel. I just thought I'd ask you first since I haven't seen you in a long time."

"Of course you can stay with me," Carol insisted. "Actually, you might want to buy my house. I have decided to move to Florida to be close to Andrea. She's going to have a baby in November. You're going to be a great-aunt! When will you be moving?"

Nancy was speechless for a moment, "Andrea's having a baby? Wow, that's exciting news! I'm so happy for her. I wish my baby brother could be around to see his little girl become a mother."

"I know, me too," Carol said. "He would have been a wonderful grandfather. He was always so proud of everything Andrea did. She's definitely her daddy's girl. I'm sure he's looking down from heaven and smiling at her."

"I know he is," Nancy agreed. She remembered why she had called, "Oh, so the reason for my call...Roger's supposed to start work in the Portland office in mid-August, so we're hoping to find something soon. When are you moving to Florida?"

"I'm not sure yet, but right around the same time you're moving. Andrea asked me to try to be down there before she is in her last trimester."

"Oh, I see. That's quite a move," Nancy said. "We were planning to fly up to Portland next weekend to look for houses. We could still come and discuss your house, as well as looking at a few others. The thing is that we are just going to rent since after the first year, Roger has the option of staying in Portland, or coming back to Texas."

"Nancy, this is a perfect situation. If you and Roger are interested, I would be happy to rent the house to you for a year. We could do it on a lease option. Stay with me next weekend. You can look things over, talk about it and let me know. I've just started to get the house ready to list. I definitely won't have it ready to list before then."

"Great," Nancy agreed. "We'll book the flight and let you know when we're arriving. It'll be so nice to see you."

♥

The months were full of activity; between the business and personal arrangements getting ready for the move, Carol kept busy and the time flew by. She had three weeks until the move, and she had begun her final packing. Nancy and Roger would be moving in with her in a week, and she wanted to have everything packed by the time they got there, so they could start their unpacking. She was still jogging every day, and had increased to jogging two miles a day.

"Joan, everything has been falling into place. It scares me that it's all been too perfect. That isn't how life goes. I need a few glitches to happen so I know it's not a fairy tale." Carol had stopped by Joan's house on her way back from her morning jog.

"Just count your blessings, Carol. Once in a while it's ok if things just fall into place," Joan patted Carol's hand. "Don't worry, there's always time for something to go wrong. Just don't look for it or wish for it." They both laughed.

Carol stood up, "I better go take my shower and get on with my day. Let's have dinner tonight, unless you have plans with Martin. "

"I'd love to have dinner with you. Martin is still visiting his son in California," Joan responded.

"OK then, let's do that," Carol said as she turned to leave. She picked up her jacket from the chair, opened the door and said, "We'll talk about where to go later." She turned to step out the door, but tripped and fell, landing on the concrete patio. "Oh, my arm, I hurt my arm!" Carol was writhing in pain.

Joan rushed out the door to help her. "Are you alright, Carol?"

"No, I'm not! My arm hurts so bad," Carol exclaimed. "I think I must have sprained it or something." She got up with some difficulty and put on a brave face. "I'm sure it's fine. Maybe I should ice it."

"Here's that glitch you were looking for, Carol. Let me take you to emergency. Your arm is swelling."

♥

"Well, young lady, you have a fractured radial head. You'll need a splint on your arm for a couple weeks and you'll need to start exercising it to get range of motion and strength back as soon as we take the splint off. Wear the sling for five to six weeks." Carol shook her head as she listened to the doctor.

"I can't do that, Doctor. I'm moving!"

"I'm sorry, I didn't mean to imply that you had a choice," he joked with her. "Unfortunately, we can't just un-break your elbow. In fact, let's get you scheduled to see an orthopedist as soon as the splint is off. Sometimes these breaks require surgery. It's too difficult to tell how bad the break is until the swelling goes down."

"Well, shit! I knew things were going along too smoothly!" Carol looked at the doctor, "Sorry."

The doctor waved it off. "When are you moving?"

"In about three weeks, and I still have to pack. I'm moving to Florida where my daughter lives."

"You'll need to find some help with that packing. I don't want you lifting anything over fifteen or twenty pounds. You can take Advil for the pain – four pills, four times a day. I'll have my receptionist find an orthopedist in Florida. You can wait until you get down there, but you need to get in right away once you're there. "

♥

"Joan, I should have started my packing sooner. Nancy and Roger will be here in a week and I had planned to be all packed by then. How will they be able to unpack any of their boxes with me and my stuff in their way?"

Joan helped Carol in the door. "Don't worry about that right now. I'll help you with your packing. Nancy and Roger will understand. In fact, I'm sure Nancy will be happy to help you with the packing as well."

Carol was obviously frustrated, "Well the timing couldn't have been any worse."

"Oh, what would have been a good time to break your elbow?" Joan snickered.

Chapter Thirteen

Carol would be flying to Florida in the morning. With the help of Joan and Nancy, the packing had been done with time to spare. The movers had gone a week ahead of her, so all her things had already been loaded into Andrea and Jason's guesthouse.

Carol was both excited for her new life in Stuart and sad to leave her life in Tigard behind. She was glad she and Joan had made plans for a Caribbean cruise in January. Carol would also be flying back to do the photography for Monica and David's wedding in a month. So it wasn't that she would be really leaving her old life behind.

Joan and Nancy had planned a going away party for her, an afternoon barbecue. Carol was dressing for it now. She chose a pair of khaki capris and a turquoise blouse for the afternoon, and slipped on a pair of white sandals on her way out of the bedroom.

Her mother, Charlotte, had come from Spokane a few days before. She would cherish these days with her mother forever. She walked into the kitchen where her mom was just finishing washing a few dishes, and kissed her on the cheek. "Mom, you're a guest in this house. You don't need to do dishes, besides those things could have been loaded in the dishwasher."

Charlotte dried her hands and gave her daughter a hug, "There were just a few things here and I thought it would be a good idea to wash them so when the guests come, everything would be clean."

Nancy walked into the kitchen, "Charlotte, you washed dishes again, didn't you? I swear you're an impossible guest. I can't get you to stop cleaning. Now I know where Carol gets her cleaning fanaticism." She smiled and walked to the door, "The guests should be arriving soon, let's go outside." She led the ladies out to the patio where Joan and Roger were setting up chairs.

Many years ago, Carol and Jim had built their patio to adjoin Joan's so they could host mutual get-togethers. They could also close the gate, which was on rollers for privacy. They had never used the gate and had tested it a couple times a year to make sure it would still close.

Carol walked over to help with the chairs and Roger said, "We don't need your help, Lefty. Why don't you sit with Uncle Fred?" With Carol's right arm in a sling, she wasn't much help. Roger and Nancy had driven over to Cannon Beach the day before to bring Fred back for the party.

Carol sat next to Fred and kissed him on the cheek. "I'm so glad you could come, Uncle Fred! I'm going to miss my visits with you."

Fred smiled at Carol, "I thought you'd never leave! I've been trying to get rid of you for years!" Fred was always joking. He reached over and hugged her tightly. "I'll miss you, sweetheart. Make sure you come see me when you come back for visits." He had tears in his eyes, making Carol feel guilty. She was always trying to please everyone and while she wanted and needed to live near her daughter, she felt like she was abandoning those she was leaving behind in the northwest.

Fred took Carol's hand, "You and Jim have always held a special place in my heart. I've never shared with you a conversation I had with him when he came to see me that last day. Carol, Jim doesn't want you to be alone. You need to find a good man to take care of you the way Jim wanted to."

Carol's thoughts went to Andrew, and once again she didn't know how he kept popping into her head. "Fred, I'm just not interested in finding someone. I suppose when the time is right, I'll know. I just still miss Jim, and I can't imagine being with someone else." She put her head on Fred's shoulder, and they sat quietly enjoying each other's company.

Guests started arriving then, and it was a fantastic afternoon with family and friends. Carol felt loved and knew she would miss them all. The day went by quickly and Carol thanked everyone for making her feel special.

♥

Andrea and Jason picked Carol up at the airport in West Palm Beach and they talked non-stop on the drive to Stuart. Andrea had planned on a light dinner at home, and Carol agreed.

"I feel so badly about your arm, Mom. Does it hurt?" Andrea asked as they were driving away from the airport.

"It mostly only hurts when I'm doing the exercises now. Quite frankly, it's just a pain in the ass that I'm not able to do any lifting."

"We'll help you with all your unpacking. In fact, don't do any of it without us to help you," Jason interjected. "I'll do all the lifting and you can tell me where to put everything..." He turned his head toward the ladies, "That's not quite what I meant to say."

"No, I think I heard you right...you want me to tell you where to put it?" They all laughed.

They arrived home before they knew it, and as Andrea and Carol walked toward the house, Jason walked to the trunk of the car to retrieve Carol's bags to carry them in. Andrea said, "I want you to stay in the main house with us for now, Mom." She unlocked the door and held it open as Carol and Jason walked in.

"Don't be silly, Andy. It's just a little break."

"I don't care how little the break is, Mom. At least until we know if you will need surgery on it let us take care of you."

"Fine, my appointment with the orthopedist is on Wednesday. I'll stay in the main house until then. Right now, I'm starving. What did you have planned for dinner? I'll help you."

As they started dinner, Carol was watching her daughter. "Andrea, you are absolutely glowing. You must be the most beautiful pregnant woman of all time," Carol exclaimed. "And it's not that I'm prejudiced or anything."

"I'd have to agree with you completely, Carol, and I'm totally unbiased as well," Jason said. He looked at Carol, "That's what I tell her all the time. Her little baby bump is adorable." Jason walked up behind his wife wrapping his arms around her, gently rubbing her belly and kissed her cheek.

"Oh, stop it, you two," Andrea said, blushing. "You're embarrassing me!"

They made a quick dinner of sandwiches and soup, and ate it on the patio. It was a nice evening, but there were clouds looming to the east and the wind was picking up as they were finishing dinner.

Chapter Fourteen

Andrea drove Carol to the orthopedist on Wednesday morning. The appointment went quickly. Carol's elbow was x-rayed and she was told it was healing nicely and wouldn't require any surgery. The orthopedist referred Carol to a physical therapist and they were on their way.

"That went very well," Carol said. She looked over at Andrea, "Now I'd like to go car shopping if you don't mind."

"I don't mind at all, Mom. Where would you like to go? Do you have something in mind?"

"Yes, I do," Carol responded with a big smile. "Your father and I always talked about buying a Mercedes Benz and we never got around to doing it."

"I don't think there's a Mercedes dealership in Stuart, but we can go to the one in Fort Pierce." They drove up US 1 to Fort Pierce, and when they arrived at the dealership, Carol spotted the car she wanted immediately. Getting out of Andrea's car, she made sure she looked at other cars instead so that nobody would see that she was interested in the red convertible.

A salesman came out to greet them. Carol and Andrea were both taken aback when they saw him because he bore an uncanny resemblance to Jim. "Good morning, ladies," he extended his right hand. "My name is Eddie, and you are?"

Carol reached with her left hand since her right arm was in the sling. "I'm Carol, and this is my daughter, Andrea." She expected to hear the typical 'you're not old enough to be her mother' and was pleasantly surprised when Eddie didn't say it. Carol and Andrea exchanged a look of disbelief at how much Eddie reminded them of Jim. The look was not lost on Eddie.

"Carol, Andrea, it's a pleasure. Is there something wrong? I couldn't help but notice the way you just looked at each other."

Carol shook her head slowly, "I'm sorry, Eddie, it's just that you look so much like my husband."

"Well, then he must be a very likeable fellow. I bet he's a great guy," Eddie said, with a grin.

Andrea said, "My father was a wonderful man. Unfortunately, we lost him in a car accident four years ago."

"I'm so sorry to hear that," Eddie said, a little uncomfortable now. He changed the subject and looked at Carol, "How can I help you today?"

"I was thinking about buying a car. I'm undecided about whether I want a Mercedes or a Porsche though," Carol told him. She glanced quickly at Andrea.

Eddie asked Carol the appropriate questions and started showing her some cars. She kept bringing the conversation back to Porsche to let him know that she still needed to be sold, and to ensure she would get a good deal. She drove a couple different cars, acting rather undecided for a while. After wheeling and dealing, Carol drove off the lot in a brand new Metallic Storm Red CLK 550 Cabriolet convertible, the very car she spotted when they drove onto the lot. She got an excellent deal on the car.

Carol and Andrea had agreed to meet at Olive Garden for a late lunch on the way back to Stuart. After they were seated, Andrea said, "You didn't mention that you were also interested in a Porsche, Mom. I would have driven you to West Palm and you could have looked at Porsches and Mercedes there."

Carol smiled, "I didn't want to get a Porsche. I was just using that as a bargaining tool. I figured if I let them know I had interest elsewhere, I would get a better deal."

"I had no idea you were so good at this car negotiation thing," Andrea giggled.

"Well, I don't know if it helped, but I figured it couldn't hurt. I did get a great deal," She hesitated before asking, "Could you believe how much that salesman looked like your father?"

"He did have an incredible resemblance," Andrea agreed. They finished their lunch and drove back to the house in their separate cars.

♥

The next morning, Carol stopped by Andrew's office to sign the paperwork for the insurance policy on her new car. "You didn't waste any time finding a new car, Carol," Andrew said when he greeted her. They chatted like old friends catching up on each other's lives. "What's on your agenda today?"

Carol glanced at the time, "I'm actually on my way to physical therapy. I don't mean to be rude, but I better run. I've only got a few minutes to get there," she said as she opened the door. "It was great to see you, Andrew. Talk to you later." With that she was gone.

Andrew had hoped they would be able to talk more. He had thought about her a lot over the past couple of months and he was hoping to see more of her and be able to get to know her better.

Carol drove the few blocks to the physical therapy office on Ocean Boulevard, and parked her new car in what she thought would be the safest spot. The appointment went better than she thought it would as she had been dreading being put through torture by the physical therapist She had been surprised that she was able to get an appointment so soon. The therapist mostly had her doing the same exercises the doctor in Oregon had told her to do when her splint was taken off. The hour went by quickly and she was soon walking back to her car.

"Carol, how's that new car?" It was Eddie, the Mercedes salesman from the day before walking toward her.

"Eddie, what a surprise! The new car is great. Thank you for asking. So, is this a part of the service that Mercedes provides? Do you have a tracking device on the car so you can find your customers the day after they buy from you to see how they like the car?" Carol laughed.

Eddie chuckled, "Now that's a great idea! I'll have to borrow that one. Actually, my barber is across the street. I have the day off and I thought I should make myself more presentable. I was starting to get a little shaggy. What are you up to today?"

Carol indicated her arm which was still in the sling. "Today was my first physical therapy appointment. So I just spent the last hour being tortured and I'm actually paying for it," she joked.

"That doesn't sound like any fun. Say, it's noon and I'm hungry. Will you join me for lunch? There's a great pizza place just a block away."

Carol thought for a moment, "It's very kind of you to offer, Eddie, but I hate to impose."

"It's not imposing if you're invited, Carol. I would really like it if you shared lunch with me...oh, you don't like pizza, do you? Well we can go someplace else if you'd like."

"Oh, I love pizza and I'd like to share a pizza with you, Eddie, just no anchovies!" Carol said. They walked down the block to the pizzeria, making small talk on the way.

The lunch crowd hadn't arrived yet, so they found a table quickly and ordered a pizza and sodas. They had just begun eating when Carol noticed Brad and Angie Potter come into the restaurant. She waved to them, "Brad, Angie, how are you? It's good to see you."

The couple walked over to the table Carol and Eddie were sharing, looking Eddie up and down. Angie said, "Carol, how is your arm? Andrea told me you broke your elbow."

"It's healing just fine. I'm just a little impatient with it because I want to be able to do more. It's hard not being able to lift things. And I'm right handed, so writing is difficult." She remembered Eddie was sitting next to her, "Oh, I'm sorry…Eddie, this is Brad and Angie Potter. They were my daughter and son-in-law's neighbors for several years." She looked at Angie and Brad, "Eddie sold me my new car. I bought a Mercedes yesterday. In fact, your dad wrote the insurance policy, Brad."

Eddie stood up and extended his hand, "Brad, Angie, it's a pleasure. Would you two like to sit with us?"

Brad started to say no, but before he could, Angie said, "That would be wonderful."

Angie sat down and Brad started toward the front counter for a menu. Before he got very far Eddie suggested, "We have more than enough pizza here if you don't mind the fact that it has cooled a bit. Unless Carol wants to take it home, it's just going to get thrown out when we leave. Just get something to drink for yourselves."

"I'm not taking any pizza with me. I don't want it on the seat of my new car," Carol insisted.

Brad hesitated, and then said, "Alright, I don't like to be a freeloader, but if you're sure. Can I get you two a refill on your sodas?"

"I'm fine, Brad, thank you," Carol said.

Eddie said, "I'm good, my friend."

The group enjoyed their pizza and talked mostly about cars, Mercedes in particular. Carol noticed that Brad seemed to be sizing Eddie up and down, and she wondered what that was about. When they had eaten all the pizza, they realized that the time had gotten away from them. They left the pizzeria and parted company.

Eddie walked Carol back to her car. "Carol, can I take you to dinner Saturday night? There's a great place down in Jupiter that I think you would like, The Crab House. I promise not to keep you out late. I have to be up early the next morning anyway to catch a flight up to New York. We can make an early evening of it." He had taken her hand in his.

Carol looked at her hand and then up to Eddie's face, before answering him, "I suppose that would be alright." She took her hand back.

"Well, don't let me twist your arm," Eddie joked. "Sorry, considering the condition of your arm, that was a terrible expression. I'll pick you up at five thirty, if that's o.k. with you."

Carol smiled a little apprehensively, "That's fine, Eddie. I'm sorry. I'm not used to going to dinner with men. I haven't spent any time alone with a man since my husband died."

Eddie patted her hand, "I promise to be a perfect gentleman. Why don't you write your address down for me?" He reached into his pocket for one of his business cards and a pen and handed them both to Carol. She wrote the address on the card, handing them back to him.

When Carol walked in the door at Andrea and Jason's house, Andrea turned to look at her, "I hear you had a lunch date."

Carol stopped in her tracks and looked at Andrea, "Wherever did you hear that? It wasn't a lunch date. I ran into Eddie…you know…the Mercedes salesman. It was lunch time, so he asked if I wanted to grab a pizza with him. It wasn't a date."

Andrea giggled, "Don't get so defensive, Mom. Angie called me and told me that she and Brad went for pizza and you were there with a man. She said they sat with you…so do you like Eddie?"

Suddenly Carol felt really silly that she had agreed to go to dinner with Eddie. "He's a nice man, but if you're asking if I like him romantically, the answer is no. I'm not at a stage where I can feel that way about a man." Carol had started tidying the kitchen, "Oh, by the way, Eddie asked me to have dinner with him Saturday night. You and Jason will be free of me that evening."

Andrea raised her eyebrows, looking at her mother with all kinds of questions in mind, but didn't say a word.

Chapter Fifteen

Carol wanted to call Eddie to cancel dinner, but she had waited too long to call because of her indecisiveness. She now had about an hour until he would be here to pick her up and she knew she couldn't cancel now. Why had she agreed to go to dinner with him? She was feeling very uncomfortable with this. Maybe she could pretend that she suddenly came down with stomach flu. *Get a grip, Carol,* she told herself. *You're an adult. Act like one.*

She decided to just make the best of it. She chose a flowered sleeveless dress and a light blue cardigan to wear for the evening. She slipped her feet into soft brown leather woven slingback sandals and scrutinized herself in the mirror. She thought she had achieved the look she was going for, matronly and classy, and not at all like she was trying to impress anyone.

She walked out of her bedroom and went looking for Andrea. She found her with Jason in the nursery. Andrea had asked Jason to rearrange the furniture yet again. "Andrea, your poor husband has rearranged this room a half dozen times now. Jason, you're a saint," Carol said. She turned and posed, "I'm ready for my dinner. How do I look?"

Jason said, "You look fine, Carol."

"This is probably the first time 'fine' was the look I was going for," Carol laughed.

"Mom, seriously, you're wearing that for a date? You look beautiful, but you look like you're going to a book club. I know you haven't been on a date in like a hundred years, but that's not a date dress."

Carol smiled, "Thank you both, it seems I have gotten the results I was looking for when I dressed for this dinner which, by the way, is not a date."

"Live in denial if you must, Mother," Andrea giggled. "Like I said, you look beautiful…as always." And then as Carol walked away, she said softly, "It's still a date."

Jason nodded his head in agreement, and then looked at Andrea, "Does it bother you to see you mom going on a date?"

She shook her head, "No, not really. It's weird, because it's new. But I don't want her to be alone, and I know Daddy wouldn't want her to be alone…" She paused pensively, "I think what bothers me is that I wanted her to hook up with Andrew."

♥

After Carol and Eddie were seated outside, overlooking the Loxahatchee River, Carol said, "This is lovely, what a nice view of the lighthouse and the river." She was still amazed at how much Eddie looked like Jim, and was doing her best to keep from looking at him too much. She certainly didn't want to give the wrong impression.

Eddie smiled, "The food is always good here." Looking directly into Carol's eyes he added, "I like to come here from time to time, but the company, and the view, is especially nice tonight."

Carol blushed and looked at her hands which were folded in her lap, uncomfortable under his gaze. This was feeling too much like a date. Andrea was right, she was in denial. This was a date! She was relieved that the waiter appeared at that moment.

"Would you like to hear the specials this evening?"

They listened to the specials and ordered. When the waiter walked away, Carol said, "Eddie, are you a native Floridian?"

"No, I'm from New York…me and half the population of Southern Florida," he said. "I moved here thirty some years ago after I graduated high school."

"Really? I don't hear a New York accent."

"Yeah, I pretty much lost my accent and don't sound like a New Yorker anymore, except when I get back from a visit. I'm going up there for a week, and when I get back, I'll sound like a New Yorker again for a little while."

Carol was glad to know that Eddie would be gone for a while. That meant he wouldn't be able to ask for a second date right away, that's assuming he would even want to. It was perfect that he was going to be gone for a week because she was going to Oregon in ten days to photograph Monica and David's wedding.

Eddie broke into her thoughts, "Maybe we can go to a movie or something when I get back from New York."

Carol looked at him and said, "Well, it sounds like you'll be back right around the time I'm going back to Oregon to shoot a wedding. Sorry, I don't think that'll work"

"Ah, well, we'll figure something out."

Carol changed the subject, "So, Eddie, do you have any children?"

"No, I've never been married," he said. "No children out of wedlock either...that I know of," he joked. "Seriously, any past girlfriends would have told me if there was a child. I've never been the playboy type. No one night stands or anything."

Carol thought he was sharing more than she needed to know and regretted asking the question. She also thought he might be sugar coating his story to make a good impression. Things had definitely changed since she'd been single. Well, she'd never really been single. She was only fifteen when she and Jim had started dating.

Eddie seemed to sense her discomfort and changed the subject, "So, Carol, when is your daughter's baby due?"

Eddie had no way of knowing that he had picked the perfect question to ease Carol's tension. Her face lit up, "She's due the day after Thanksgiving. We're really going to have something to be thankful for this year! She's having a girl, and naming her Jamie Grace. They're naming her after my husband and Jason's grandmother. I never thought I would be this excited to be a grandmother. The baby is the main reason I decided to move to Florida...oh, I wanted to be near my daughter, but I also wanted to be where I can spoil my granddaughter more often." Her smile had grown as she was talking, "Oh, this is probably boring for you."

"Not at all. Just because I don't have kids of my own doesn't mean I don't like them. I grew up in a large Irish-Catholic family. Kids are always the center of holidays in my family. Are you planning to live with your daughter, or is that just temporary?"

"I'll be moved into the guest house in the next couple days, which had been the plan since they bought their place. But when I got here with my arm in a sling, they convinced me to stay at their house for a bit. Andrea and Jason have been helping me get unpacked before I move over there. I'll be looking for my own house, but I'm sure the guest house will be so comfortable that there is no hurry. It'll be nice for Andrea to have a built-in babysitter at first anyway."

"I would think a built-in babysitter was a great asset," Eddie said. "You better be careful they don't take advantage of that."

"They wouldn't take advantage. I'm so excited to have a granddaughter, I probably wouldn't notice if they did. In fact, they'll probably have a hard time getting rid of me. And to think they had to convince me to move to Florida in the first place."

Carol relaxed after that, and the rest of the evening went better than the first part had. They enjoyed a tasty dinner and pleasant conversation, along with perfect weather for an outdoor meal. The drive back to Stuart was a pleasant one. When they arrived at the house, Eddie walked Carol to the door and she became a little tense again, not knowing what to expect.

With her right arm in the sling, Carol extended her left hand to Eddie, "Thank you for dinner, Eddie, I had a nice time."

Eddie took her hand and brought it up to his lips and kissed it, "The pleasure was mine, Carol. Can I call you when I get back from New York?"

"I'd like that, Eddie." She was surprised that she actually meant it.

♥

The following morning, Carol woke up earlier than normal and decided to drive over the Intracoastal to Hutchinson Island and jog on the beach. She'd been jogging St. Lucie Boulevard starting from the house since she arrived in Florida. On this particular morning, she decided a jog on the beach was in order. There were no other cars in the lot when she pulled in. She got out of her car and walked out to the beach, stretching before starting her jog. The sun was just coming up, and she realized she was experiencing her first Florida sunrise.

Her run was enjoyable, watching the sun coming up and the waves rolling in. Running on the sand gave her a different workout than those she got from running on pavement. She was truly enjoying the morning and decided to stop for a while and take the time to appreciate the quiet morning. She sat in the sand and watched the waves, thinking about all the changes in her life.

She thought back to the letter Jim had written to her just months before he died. "Am I doing O.K. now, Jim?" She asked out loud, feeling happy and more fulfilled than she had at any time since Jim's death. She wished he could talk to her though. She thought he would be pleased with her progress. But she felt guilty about her dinner the night before and it still didn't feel right to even think about dating.

No sense brooding over that right now. She stood up to finish her run. She started back in the direction she had come from, relishing the early morning ocean air. She wondered why she hadn't come to the beach to run when she first arrived in Florida.

Carol was nearing the parking lot when she saw a jogger coming from the other direction. As he grew closer, she realized it was Andrew and her heart skipped a beat. She thought, w*hat are you? 13?*

Andrew was just a few yards away now, Carol called to him in between her labored breaths, "Andrew…good morning…lovely day…isn't it?"

"That it is," he said just as he reached her, panting as well. "I thought that was…your hot red car…in the parking lot. Do you…come here to jog often?"

"No, this is the first time I've jogged here," she said, having caught her breath. "Right after I went back to Oregon in May, I started jogging again for the first time in years. You inspired me actually. It was seeing you jogging when I came here to visit Andrea that gave me the kick in the butt I needed to get off said butt," she said smiling. Andrew smiled back. "I've been jogging on St. Lucie Boulevard in front of Andrea and Jason's house since I got back here, but this morning, I thought it would be nicer to jog along the beach, and I was right!"

"Jogging on the beach is more peaceful. You know, Carol...unless you prefer to jog alone, perhaps you'll consider jogging with me once in a while."

"I'd like that, Andrew. I enjoy being alone with my thoughts part of the time, but it would be great to have a jogging companion for other times. Right now, I should get home and shower or I'll be late for church." They both turned to walk to their cars.

Andrew smiled, "Me too. Hey, if you're not doing anything later, come over to my place this afternoon. I'm having a small barbecue, just Brad and Angie and me. Bring Jason and Andrea."

"That sounds great! Let me check with them to make sure they don't have other plans. I'll call after church to let you know."

Chapter Sixteen

Carol picked up her rental car and got on I-5 headed toward Joan's house in Tigard, where she would be staying for the week. It would feel strange staying with her friend next door to her old home. She had thought about staying with Nancy and Roger, but she and Joan had a lot of catching up to do, and Joan had plenty of room.

Carol was looking forward to the salmon Joan had told her she was going to bake for dinner. She knew they would stay up late drinking wine and gossiping like they had done for years on occasion. It had only been a couple weeks since Carol left, but there was a lot to talk about. Carol pulled into Joan's driveway and it felt both familiar and bizarre.

As she turned off the car she saw Joan at the kitchen window. The door flew open and Joan rushed out. They hugged and both started talking at once. Even though they were both talking at the same time, they heard what the other said in their greetings, sounding like a couple of chickens cackling to each other in the barnyard.

"Let me get your bag, Carol. Come in…come in. You look so tan. How's your arm? Did you have a good flight? It's wonderful to see you!"

"You really don't need to carry that for me, Joan. My arm is getting better…still doing physical therapy…but, as you can see, I don't need the sling anymore. It's so good to see you, Joan!"

They both took a breath. They took Carol's things to the guest room, and Carol freshened up while Joan started the salmon. She was chopping up the vegetables for the salad when Carol walked back in the room.

"What can I do to help?" Carol asked as she reached in the cabinet for plates to set the table.

"Not a thing. Have a seat. Everything is about ready. Do you want a glass of wine?"

Carol grinned, "Like you had to ask? Of course! I'll pour us both a glass."

They chatted over dinner. They chatted while cleaning up after dinner. They chatted over the chocolate torte Joan had made for dessert. And then they chatted over more wine.

"I have exciting news," Joan suddenly said. "I couldn't decide when to tell you."

"What is it?"

"Martin and I have set a date. We're getting married."

"Joan, that's wonderful. He's a good man. What's the date?"

"January 14th. Right after you and I take our Caribbean cruise. Martin is going to fly down to greet us when we get off the boat. He and I will stay down there for that week and we've made arrangements to get married on that Thursday, which is the 14th. At our ages, we don't need a long engagement. Then we're booked for a cruise to the Bahamas."

"Joan, that's fantastic!"

"I was hoping you would take some pictures. We just want to have one really nice picture for us to have. And we will need to have a couple of witnesses."

"Of course…I'd be glad to take pictures. Andrea and Jason can be the witnesses. I'm sure they'd be happy to do it!" Carol walked around to Joan's side of the table and hugged her friend.

"Well, we're both seventy and had long marriages to our first spouses, so we don't need to have a bunch of pictures. We just thought it would be nice to have one special picture. So, tell me about what's been going on in this new chapter of your life, Carol, now that you've had the courage to turn the page."

Carol smiled. "I just got all moved into the guest house at Andrea and Jason's a couple days before coming here. With my arm in the sling, I stayed in their house and they helped me with the unpacking little by little until I had it just the way I wanted it. So when I go back in a week, everything is all ready for me."

"I hope that's not all you've been doing."

"No, of course not. I told you about my new car…I love it."

"Sweetie, that's all trivial. What have you been doing with yourself?"

Carol looked down and started wringing her hands before she looked back up at Joan. "I went on a date, Joan. I felt so guilty. And I'm so naïve that I didn't even realize it was a date until we were sitting in the restaurant. I just thought it was two people having dinner. I felt more uncomfortable than you can imagine."

Joan patted her friend's hand. "There is no reason for you to feel guilty because you went on a date. Why did you feel guilty? Did you think you were cheating on Jim? You're not cheating. Jim has been gone four years. You'd be hard pressed to find anyone in the world who would even judge you for going out to dinner with another man after all these years. In fact, if you will remember, that is what Jim wanted you to do.

"I wonder what you thought those lunches you had with that insurance man were back in May when you went to Florida. I have news for you, my dear. Those were also dates. And that's ok. You can and you should enjoy male companionship."

Carol looked at Joan, her elbows resting on the table and her chin in the palms of her hands. "When you say that, it makes sense. So…why doesn't it feel right?"

"Because it's new. You just need time to change your mindset from married woman to single woman. And follow your instincts. Maybe this guy is nice, but he might not be right for you, even on a casual basis. And remember, Carol, you never had much experience with dating. Jim was your first and only love. Dating is nothing more than getting to know someone so you can find out if you want to know them better. There is no reason to feel guilty about that. Does that make sense to you?"

"Joan, you're so wise. I feel like an adolescent when it comes to this stuff."

"You'll catch on…now tell me about this date."

"Well…ok…it was the Mercedes salesman who sold my car to me. You wouldn't believe how much he looks like Jim. It's hard for me not to stare at him. The funny thing is, even though there is such a strong resemblance, and I always thought my husband was so handsome I have no attraction to Eddie. Don't get me wrong…he is a handsome man…and he seems nice…I'm just not attracted to him. In fact, after I thought about it, I think I agreed to go to dinner with him because he kind of sold me on the date. When I looked back at our conversation in my mind, I realized that he actually closed the sale…I guess once a salesman, always a salesman."

"Well, you know the old saying…there are plenty of fish in the sea."

"The thing is… he asked me out again…he wanted me to go to dinner with him last night as a matter of fact, and I went with him but I used this trip for an excuse to come right home. Which is kind of funny because the first time we went out, he was flying home to New York the next morning, so that was an early night as well. But he's persistent and he said he'd call me when I get back."

Joan laughed softly. "Sounds like he may be smitten, kitten." They both laughed at Joan's rhyme. The wine probably made it funnier than it really was.

"Oh, Joan, you always make me laugh."

"What else have you been doing with yourself?"

"I'm still jogging every morning. In fact, I've started to take some of my runs on the beach. I even have a jogging companion three days a week. He's the insurance man I told you about…the father of Andrea and Jason's old neighbors. He's really a nice man." The look Joan gave Carol was lost on her as she was looking at her wine glass.

Carol poured two more glasses of wine. "Oh, I bought a new camera, and I've been taking some great pictures. I haven't decided if I'm going to start a new photography studio down there or not. I'm thinking about a few different options."

"Tell me about them," Joan said.

"Well, I've taken some really great pictures of Andrea, and some with Andrea and Jason…sort of chronicling the pregnancy. I thought about a photography business for pregnancies and babies. There are more and more people using photographers for that. And my other idea is for free lance photography, or maybe just photographing whatever I feel like photographing and selling my individual prints in local shops. I don't know…I'm not in any big hurry to make any decisions. That chapter isn't written yet," Carol said with a smile.

"Those all sound wonderful. I'm sure when the time is right for you to decide about your business, you'll do something marvelous."

They talked until well into the night.

♥

Sarah had gone to Monica and David's wedding with Carol and they were on their way back to the studio. "I'm really glad I came with you, Carol. I love watching you work. You are such a professional. I always learn something from you. I really don't know what I'm doing without you."

"Of course you do. You're very good. I could see you were a natural years ago when I hired you. The rest comes with practice and experimentation. Never be afraid to try new things…think outside the box…shoot outside the box. Do things…take pictures you've never seen other photographers take." Carol smiled at Sarah. Sarah was a very good photographer, and she had a great future in photography.

"How can I ever thank you for all you've done for me? You gave me the best job as soon as I graduated from community college and you've allowed me to buy into your business. You've basically given me a future."

"You've worked hard for it, and I didn't give you a future. It's been wonderful to see your growth as a photographer. Now, tell me what else is going on in your life. Don't fall into the trap I did and make the business too important."

"Oh Carol, Tom and I are trying to get pregnant. We decided we can't put it off any longer. I'll be 29 next month. So we figured we better start cooking while the eggs are still fresh."

Carol smiled at Sarah's analogy. "Good for you! You know what? Rebecca has been doing a great job, but maybe it's time to add another assistant…"

♥

The week had gone much too quickly. Carol would be leaving the next morning. She and Joan had driven over to Cannon Beach to see Uncle Fred. They took Fred to Camp 18 for lunch and couldn't resist sharing one of their delicious, but monstrous, cinnamon rolls.

"I am completely stuffed. I'm going to have to jog twenty miles in the morning if I'm going to fit on the plane," Carol said as they were walking back to the car.

"I'm really glad you came to see me. I've missed your visits," Uncle Fred said with his arm around Carol. "I hope you'll come back to see me the next time you're in Oregon."

"You know I will, Uncle Fred."

Carol drove Fred home, promising to be back for a visit as soon as she could, before driving back over Highway 26. They were just reaching the exit to take 217 down to Tigard when Carol's phone started to ring.

"Joan, will you answer that for me?" She asked handing her phone to Joan.

Joan took the phone and glanced at the caller ID. "Oh, it's Andrea." Joan answered and Carol pulled off the road in case the call was something serious. She pulled into a parking lot and realized by hearing Joan's side of the conversation that Andrea wasn't calling about anything bad.

"OK Sweetie, it's been wonderful talking to you. I'm going to hand you off to your mom, who is staring at me impatiently. Take care of yourself, and that precious bundle. I'll see you in January." Joan handed the phone to Carol, who stuck her tongue out at her.

"I was not looking at you impatiently," she said with a smile as she held the phone to her ear. "What's going on, Andy?"

"Hi, Mom. I'm fine…how are you?" Andrea said laughing. "I just wanted to let you know that Andrew is going to pick you up at the airport tomorrow. He told me he had to be in West Palm Beach anyway and offered to pick you up. I hope you don't mind."

"Of course I don't mind. It doesn't make sense for you to drive down to pick me up when he needs to be there anyway. What is Andrew doing in West Palm tomorrow?"

"You know…I didn't even ask."

"Are you feeling OK?"

"Yes, I feel great. I'll let you go now."

"See you tomorrow evening, Andy."

Chapter Seventeen

"Are you hungry, Carol? Let's stop for dinner somewhere."

"That sounds nice, Andrew. I'll just call Andrea first to make sure I won't spoil any plans." Carol called Andrea while Andrew loaded Carol's bag into the trunk of his car. It had been raining all day in South Florida, and had just let up about an hour before. The clouds were breaking up and the blue skies were coming through.

"Look at this, Andrew! I've turned the gray skies blue by returning to Florida."

Andrew smiled, "You sure have." *In more ways than one*, he thought. "So are we on for dinner, or do you have to make it home before curfew," he joked. They both laughed and got in the car.

"You're quite the comedian today," Carol said, as she playfully socked him in the shoulder. "Dinner would be great."

"Perfect! Since the weather has made a turn for the better, how 'bout we stop off in Jupiter and go to Guanabanas?"

"I'd love that," Carol replied.

"Did you have a nice time in Portland?"

"Yes, it was great to see everyone, and the wedding I did the photography for was beautiful. The bride was really happy that I came back to do her wedding. Oh, and speaking of weddings, my dear friend, Joan, told me she is getting married in January. Isn't it wonderful that even in their seventies, they found love?" Carol looked pensively out her window, smiling. Andrew looked over at her and smiled too. They rode most of the rest of the way to Jupiter in a companionable silence, just making small talk now and then.

Andrew pulled up to the valet station at Guanabanas and they both got out of the car. "This looks even more beautiful than when we came for lunch," Carol exclaimed. Andrew thought Carol also looked more beautiful than when they had come there for lunch. The hostess seated them and Carol said, "Andrew, let me pay for dinner. It was so nice of you to pick me up from the airport. The least I can do is buy dinner for you."

Andrew looked at Carol and smiled, "A gentleman never lets a lady pay for dinner."

The waitress came to take their orders. Andrew ordered a rib eye steak. "I'll have the Grilled Tequila Lime Chicken," Carol said, handing the menu to the waitress. When the waitress walked away Carol said, "Andrew, I never asked the reason you had to be in West Palm today."

Andrew took a drink of his beer and looked at Carol, "To pick up a friend from the airport."

"But…I thought…Andrea said you had to be in West Palm for something anyway."

"The truth is that I realize I have some competition and I wanted to make some points."

"What do you mean, you have competition?"

"You know…the car salesman. He's vying for your attention too," he said sheepishly.

"Andrew, I'm at a place in my life where all I need are friends. I'm definitely not looking for a relationship. If that's what you want, you're barking up the wrong tree. I like you a lot, and I think we have a really nice friendship, but I'm just not ready for anything more."

Andrew felt a little bit like a school boy who had just been scolded, but he recovered quickly and said, "Of course, Carol, I think we have a beautiful friendship. I just hope to be first in line when you are ready for more than a friendship. It seems like we not only enjoy each other's company, but that we are comfortable with each other. That may not sound romantic, but I think it's wonderful. If nothing else, though, I really do want your friendship"

Carol was almost staring open mouthed at Andrew. "I guess I just didn't realize you felt that way, Andrew. You know…I really just do want your friendship right now. I've made a lot of changes in my life, and I don't feel like I'm ready for any other changes. My friend, Joan, really had to coach me on moving on to this new chapter of my life, and I am just trying to take things page by page. It's taken me four years to learn that I can enjoy life without my husband. A relationship is way more than I can handle."

Andrew patted Carol's hand, "I respect that, Carol." He extended his right hand, "Friends?"

She smiled and reached to shake his hand, "Of course! Thank you, Friend!"

♥

Carol was dressing for dinner. Eddie had called her earlier that day and asked her to go to dinner with him. Even though she really would have preferred to stay home, she decided she needed to have a talk with him, similar to the talk she'd had with Andrew. She wasn't looking forward to it, but figured since it had gone so well with Andrew she would have dinner with Eddie and get it out of the way with him. She hoped it would go even half as well.

It made her more nervous to think about having this conversation with Eddie, probably because her comfort level with him was nowhere near as high as it was with Andrew. However, she felt like there was less to lose with Eddie.

They had planned an outing at Hurricane Grill for beer and wings. Carol had dressed in denim capris and a green sleeveless blouse. She was just about to get her sweater from the closet when she heard a knock at the door, and she walked over to open it.

"Eddie, come in. I just need to get a sweater. How was your day?"

"What do you need a sweater for?"

"I get chilly in restaurants. They always blast the air conditioning."

"Are you jet lagged from your trip," Eddie asked.

"Not too bad. It's much easier coming this way…going the other way I feel like I'm losing a few hours because of the time zone changes."

"Oh, yeah, that's true. What time did you get in last night?"

Carol had her sweater in her hand and was reaching for her purse. "My flight got in at five thirty. Andrew picked me up at the airport and we stopped off in Jupiter for dinner. I think I got home around nine."

"Andrew?! The insurance guy?! What was he doing picking you up?!" Eddie shouted.

Carol was shocked, "What are you yelling about, Eddie?"

"I don't like this guy spending so much time with you!"

"I don't care what you like, Eddie! I can have whoever I want for a friend. You have nothing to say about it. I want you to leave right now," Carol said as she walked to the door and opened it. "Get out!"

"Carol…"

"GET OUT!"

Eddie reluctantly walked out the door. He started to say something when he passed her, but she turned her head away from him and he kept going. Carol firmly closed the door as soon as Eddie was out. She heard his car start up, and drive away.

♥

The next morning Carol went for a jog alone on the beach. She ran twice as far as she usually did. She felt that she needed the peace and tranquility she always got from being near the ocean and the exercise certainly couldn't hurt either. The previous evening had been really traumatic for her. She didn't understand what had gotten into Eddie. He had nothing to be jealous about. She certainly had never given him reason to believe he had any right to be jealous about anything concerning her.

She would probably never hear from him again, and that suited her just fine. She wished she had followed her instincts and turned him down the first time he had asked her to dinner. Oh well, she could put that in the past now.

When Carol got out of the shower later she was feeling much better about things. Her morning run had definitely improved her outlook. She thought she would ask Andrea if she wanted to go shopping with her after she got off work. In the meantime, she would go buy some fabric to make a pink quilt for a Jamie Grace.

At the fabric store, Carol ran into Anna, from Treasure Coast Paradise Inn. Anna invited Carol to come back to the inn for lunch. The two of them shared a lovely afternoon. Carol booked the inn for the afternoon of Andrea's baby shower, which was still more than a month away. It was scheduled for a Sunday afternoon almost three weeks before Andrea's due date.

When it was time for Carol to leave, she hugged Anna. "I'm so glad I ran into you. I've had a wonderful afternoon. Let's do this again. Next time, why don't you come to my place?"

♥

Carol took Andrea to the Treasure Coast Mall later that afternoon. She bought several outfits in different sizes for the baby, as well as some receiving blankets, onesies, sleepers, rattles, baby bottles, and everything else she could think of the baby would need. After that she bought Andrea a new maternity dress.

"Let's go for a mani-pedi, Andy…oh, is that safe during pregnancy?"

Andrea giggled, "You have to know that I asked my doctor about that! She said it's fine…no harm to me or the baby!"

They enjoyed the rest of the afternoon at the salon and took their treasures home. Carol helped Andrea put everything away in the nursery and they were just finishing when Jason got home. The bags on the nursery floor were the only source of evidence of their shopping trip when Jason walked in. There were almost enough bags to carpet the floor.

"Wow! What happened?" Jason laughed.

"Mom needed some shopping therapy this afternoon. I think Jamie has more than enough clothes to last her the first year," Andrea said. She gave her husband a kiss on the cheek, "How was your day, Jace?"

"I thought it was good, but it obviously didn't compare to yours. Carol, is there a reason you needed shopping therapy? Or were you just overdue?" He joked.

Carol told them both about the episode with Eddie the night before. "But now I've had a great day, and all is right with the world again!

Chapter Eighteen

It was warmer than usual for October, with record setting high temperatures. Their morning jog had been hot and muggy, and the sky was filled with clouds. Carol and Andrew had just gotten back to their cars when it started to sprinkle.

"We couldn't have timed that any better, could we, Andrew?"

"I don't suppose we could have," Andrew said. They had continued their morning jogs together and their friendship had grown tremendously. "Do you want to go see that new Vince Vaughn movie tonight?"

"Couples Retreat? I'd love to. His movies are always funny. I'll check the times and call you later." The sprinkle was quickly becoming more, so they both got in their cars and drove home.

When Carol arrived home, the rain was coming down in sheets, and she ran for the door, completely drenched by the time she got inside. She thought if she'd just had her soap and shampoo outside, she could have had her shower done on the way into the house. Before going in to take her shower, Carol got a small glass of orange juice and checked her phone for messages.

After showering, Carol put on a pair of pink and gray striped lounge pants and a white t-shirt and made some tea. She thought it was a perfect morning to curl up in her favorite chair with a good book and mint tea. She had purchased Nicholas Sparks' latest book *The Last Song* and hadn't taken the time to read it yet. She grabbed the book and her tea, tossed a cozy afghan onto her chair and sat down to read.

The storm outside persisted, thunder and lightning added to the mood enhancing weather. Carol loved a good thunder storm. She'd been reading in her chair for over two hours and the storm was starting to let up. Her friend, Anna, was coming for lunch and Carol realized she needed to get the quiche started.

She had planned to have a spinach and feta cheese quiche and melons for lunch. Anna was such a great cook that Carol was a little nervous to cook for her. After lunch, they were going to share some quilting ideas. Carol had finished the quilt she had made for Andrea, and was going to start on a quilt for a wedding gift for Joan and Martin.

Carol prepared the quiche and put it in the oven, and then cut up the melons. She put the bowl of melons in the refrigerator. Unfolding the baby's quilt, she laid it over the back of the sofa to show it to Anna later. Then she got out the fabric and pattern she was going to use for Joan and Martin's quilt as well.

Anna arrived just before the quiche was ready to come out of the oven. She had brought her current quilting projects, as well as a bottle of blackberry wine with her. "Carol, whatever you're making for lunch smells wonderful!"

"It's a spinach and feta cheese quiche. The blackberry wine should be great with it. I had planned to have lunch on the patio, Mother Nature obviously had other plans," she joked. "Anna, I'm so nervous for you to try my cooking. You're such a fantastic cook that for you to eat my cooking is like Julia Child eating at McDonalds," Carol said as she retrieved the melons from the refrigerator and set the bowl on the kitchen counter.

Anna laughed, "Carol, you're so funny…I'm sure you are a wonderful cook. And I'm only a good cook because I cook so much. The quiche smells great…I can't wait to try it."

Carol took the quiche from the oven and set it on the counter next to the melons and the aroma filled the room. She had set the table earlier, but got a couple of wine glasses from the cabinet. "Anna, do you want to open the wine?" Carol said as she cut the quiche.

When they were both seated, they noticed the rain had stopped and the sun was beginning to shine. "Well, it looks like Mother Nature has a great sense of humor," Anna said, taking a bite of the quiche. The look on her face showed that she liked it. "Carol, this is delicious! You have to share this recipe with me so I can use it at the bed and breakfast."

"Of course I'll share it with you, Anna." When they were done eating, they poured another glass of wine and walked into the great room. "The quilt I made for Andrea's baby is done," Carol said, indicating the quilt resting on the sofa.

Anna picked it up to inspect it as quilters do, "Carol, this is lovely. It's so soft and girly. Jamie Grace is a lucky baby…" The phone rang just then.

"Excuse me a minute, Anna," Carol said as she answered the phone. "Hello."

"Good morning, Carol. It's Sarah."

"Sarah, how are you?"

"Great, I just wanted to call you because I'm registering for a photography workshop in Dallas in a couple weeks. I thought you might like to go and we can share a hotel room. It's a three day workshop the last week of this month," Sarah explained.

"That sounds great. Will you register for both of us? Tell me the dates, and I'll book a flight."

They talked about the business. Sarah had hired a new assistant as Carol had suggested. Carol asked if there was any baby news yet. There wasn't. Carol told Sarah she had company, and would call her later to solidify their plans.

♥

Carol carried her camera equipment into the house. She had just returned from Jupiter, where she had gone to take pictures at the Jupiter Lighthouse. When she climbed to the top of the lighthouse, she was glad that she was in good shape. There were others in the tour group who had a hard time catching their breath after the climb.

The view from the top was great. The ocean waves were particularly spectacular, which made for some great photographs. When they climbed back down, the banyan tree at the base of the lighthouse provided a nice subject for more pictures. Carol had always had an appreciation for lighthouses and was considering doing a photo book of lighthouses. Florida had its share of lighthouses.

She put her camera away and was about to open the door to walk over and see if Andrea wanted to go for a walk, when the phone rang. She was shocked to find Eddie on the line. "Eddie, this is a surprise."

"I know. I wasn't sure I should call, but I finally talked myself into it. I've wanted to apologize for my behavior when I was at your house. It's taken me so long, because I really embarrassed myself and I feel ashamed of my actions. I'm not excusing my behavior, but I feel the need to explain. I had a bad day at work, and then found out my best friend has cancer. I probably should have stayed home. When you mentioned that other guy, I felt like I was losing a friend. I'm really sorry about the way I acted."

Carol was silent, not knowing how to respond. She knew she needed to be careful concerning this situation. Eddie's behavior had been deplorable and she didn't want him to think she would accept such behavior. She also didn't want to be an unforgiving person. She didn't appreciate being put in this position. Yet, she wanted to be sympathetic regarding Eddie's friend.

"Carol, will you let me buy you lunch to make it up? I'm off work tomorrow, and I was hoping we could meet for lunch. The Pelican Café?"

Carol thought for a moment. She knew she should say no, but she would have her own car, and she did feel badly about Eddie's friend. She had enjoyed his company most of the time. "OK, Eddie, I'll meet you at the Pelican Café for lunch. What time?"

♥

"I can't believe you're having lunch with him," Andrew said. They were on their morning run, and Carol had told him about her phone conversation with Eddie the day before.

"Well, I still don't know if I made the right decision but I felt that since he wanted to meet me rather than picking me up, he was sincere. If I can keep Eddie as a friend, I'll be happy."

Andrew felt jealous, but didn't let Carol know. He decided to ask her about her trip to Dallas instead, "When is your workshop in Dallas?"

"Next week. I'll fly to Dallas on Monday…the workshop is Tuesday, Wednesday, Thursday. Sarah and I will spend Friday shopping, and then I fly home on Saturday, which is Halloween...spooky, huh?" She said in the most ghoulish voice she could muster. "I'm excited for the workshop. As long as I've been in the photography business, I always learn something at them…and this will be the first time for Sarah and me to attend a workshop together. When she worked for me, I always needed her to run the shop while I was gone…and when I sent her to workshops, I had to stay at the shop. We'll have a great time."

"Just don't get soft when you're there, or I'll be running circles around you when you get back."

"Oh, you'll never run circles around me, old man," Carol said before she quickly ran a circle around him.

"Old man? Ouch...that hurts!" He grabbed her, tickling her. They both laughed and fell into the sand.

♥

The parking lot at Pelican Café was nearly full when Carol got there. The Pelican Café was an outdoor café, with walk-up ordering and picnic tables in a park-like setting, situated on the St. Lucie River. She saw Eddie sitting on top of a picnic table, as she parked her car. He smiled and waved. She got out of her car and walked over to him.

"Thank you for coming, Carol. I wouldn't have blamed you if you hadn't. I told my mother about how I acted, and she is still scolding me after a month." He extended his right hand, "Can you forgive me?"

Carol reached with her right hand, "I think I like your mother very much. You're forgiven, Eddie, but it's not forgotten."

"Understood," Eddie said. "Thank you for forgiving me. You're a wonderful woman, Carol."

Carol sat on the bench, "I hope we can be friends for a very long time, Eddie. I just want you to understand that I am not at a place in my life where I want more than friendship. I know that is difficult for men, but if you can't respect that, I'm afraid I won't be able to see you."

Eddie nodded his head, "If I didn't respect that, Carol, I'd hear it from my mother."

Carol liked the fact that his mother was so important to him. She liked the fact that his mother had such a strong influence on him even more.

"Let's order," Eddie said. "I'm starving."

Carol smiled. They walked over and ordered their lunch. They chose a table next to the river. Carol ordered fish and chips, and Eddie had a Philly cheese steak.

Carol said, "Eddie, I'm really sorry to hear about your friend. How is he doing?"

Eddie looked at Carol for a moment, "*She* is not doing well at all. Mary was diagnosed with stage four breast cancer and the prognosis isn't good. I wish I would have known when I went home for a visit, because I didn't even go see her when I was there. If I'd known about the cancer, I would have made her a top priority. I'll probably go back up there in a couple weeks so I can see her. We grew up together. Our families were neighbors. Her parents live in Vero Beach now."

"Oh, Eddie, I'm so sorry. Please let me know if there is anything I can do, even if it's just to pray with you."

"Thank you, Carol. That means a lot to me."

They ate their lunch and talked about everything, and nothing, for a couple of hours. Eddie noticed Carol look at her watch, and he checked his as well, "I've kept you too long, Carol, I'm sorry."

"It's fine, Eddie, really, but I did tell Andrea I would walk with her this afternoon. She is down to five weeks before the baby is due."

They walked to the parking lot.

"Carol, I just thought…I know this is last minute…but I'm going to a Halloween party, and I wondered if you would go with me."

"When is the party, Eddie?"

"Halloween night."

"Sorry, I won't be able to go. I'm flying home from a week in Dallas on Halloween. I can't go with you."

"That's fine, Carol. It was a last minute idea anyway."

They said good-bye and Carol felt good about where things stood between them. She had been quick to judge Eddie when they first met, and he was actually a nice guy. Although he hadn't acted in a positive way, she was glad she had given him another chance. Eddie was nothing like Jim, and the more she got to know him, the less he looked like him.

Chapter Nineteen

Andrew had been kind enough to pick Carol up from the airport and drive her home when she came back from Dallas. They went over to have dinner with Andrea and Jason. Jason made a Grim Reaper for Carol, Andrew and himself, in honor of Halloween.

When they got back to Carol's place, she asked Andrew if he wanted another Grim Reaper. They enjoyed the evening out on her patio. It was a warm night, and the company was warm as well. Andrew left when they had both finished their drinks. He knew Carol was exhausted.

The next morning, Carol slept in and decided she could skip jogging. She got up and showered, getting ready for church. She was glad she had stopped at two Grim Reapers because other than being tired she felt good.

Carol chose not to ride to church with Andrea and Jason as she and Anna had to tie up loose ends regarding the baby shower. It was just a week away now. They had decided to make it a 'couples' baby shower. Carol had wanted to invite her own mother, as well as Joan and Martin to the baby shower, but they would be coming for Thanksgiving instead.

Anna and Carol decided on the refreshments. Since the shower was scheduled for three in the afternoon, they decided on appetizers and desserts; deviled eggs, mini sandwiches, fruit and cheese trays, meat and cheese trays, angel food cake with strawberries, mini cheesecakes and mini tarts. They would have champagne, cider and coffee to drink.

Carol really liked the idea of a couples shower. It took both people to make the baby so the father should get to be a part of the whole experience. She wondered why it had taken so long for somebody to come up with the idea.

They weren't going to bother with decorations as the party would be outside. Anna and Brian had such beautiful landscaping there was no need for any decorations. They decided that less was definitely more in this case.

After they had made all the decisions regarding the baby shower, Carol went home. She hadn't unpacked from her trip to Dallas yet. She was also eager to try out some of the things she had learned at the workshop.

♥

The day before the shower had arrived, and Carol got up for her run. She drove over the Intracoastal to Stuart Beach and saw that Andrew was waiting, and stretching, when she got there. He really was a great friend.

Carol got out of her car, "I hope you weren't waiting long."

"Not long at all…I knew you'd be here soon. You have to keep running every day in order to keep up with me," he smiled at her. She loved that smile.

"Oh, really? See if you can keep up with this," she said as she took off running. She was on the beach in no time. Unfortunately for her, Andrew also caught up to her in no time.

"Guess what, Ms. Davison? Not only have I kept up with you," he said as he grabbed her waist and picked her up, "but I've passed you." He put her down and kept running, but turned and ran backwards until she regained her momentum and caught back up.

"Mr. Potter, that was way out of line. I'm afraid I'm going to have to press charges for assault," she said, laughing.

"Assault? How do you like that? I kept you from falling over your own feet…like a knight in shining armor…and you want to press charges?"

They were both laughing now.

"A knight in shining armor, huh? Wow, you have a high opinion of yourself, Mr. Potter."

They light-heartedly bantered back and forth that way for a while.

"You're still coming to the shower, right?" Carol asked.

"I wouldn't miss it. Those kids are really special. They became like family as soon as Brad and Angie bought the condo next to theirs."

"Good, I'm glad you're going to be there."

♥

The guests were starting to arrive at the baby shower, but Andrea and Jason weren't there yet. Carol was getting concerned. She had tried both their cell phones with no answer. Suddenly her phone rang, and she looked at Anna, "Finally, that's Jason calling me."

She took her phone away from the crowd to answer, "Jason, where are you two? Everyone is here."

"We're at the hospital."

"What are you doing at the hospital? The shower is right now."

"I know, Carol, but Andrea's water broke right when we were leaving for the shower. Andrea is already dilated to eight centimeters."

"Oh, tell her to wait, I'm on my way."

"Carol, it's not really under her control."

"Oh…right…I know…I'm not used to my daughter being in labor. I'll be there as soon as I can."

Carol disconnected the call and walked back to the crowd. "I want to thank you all for coming. I'm sorry but Andrea and Jason won't be able to make it…they're at the hospital having a baby…I have to go now…"

Andrew walked quickly over to Carol, "Let me drive you. We can get your car later."

"Thank you, Andrew."

They got in Andrew's car and had only gone about a block when Carol said, "Hurry, Andrew, hurry."

"I'm driving as fast as I can."

"Go around this old man."

"I am, Carol."

"Don't let that guy pull out in front of you. What are you stopping for?"

"Carol, calm down…I have to stop for the red light. You need to calm down. Andrea's in good hands," he said to her, calmly and patiently, reaching for her hand and giving it a reassuring squeeze.

"You're right, Andrew. I'm sorry. I'm just so worried...and nervous...and excited...and anxious..."

Andrew looked at Carol, smiling. She loved her daughter so much, and he realized he loved Carol.

"I know you are, but everything will be alright."

Somehow, that provided her with the composure she needed and when Andrew parked the car in the hospital parking lot, Carol walked calmly into the building with Andrew at her side. "You're a good friend, Andrew."

They were given directions to the maternity ward at the front desk. They found Andrea's room just in time. Carol gave her daughter a quick hug and kiss on the cheek before they took her to the delivery room.

"Andrew, thank you for getting me here. I probably would have caused an accident if I had driven myself here."

"I know you would have. Why do you think I wanted to drive you? Just think how many lives I saved by driving you to the hospital just now."

They walked to the waiting room, but they didn't have long to wait. They were only in the waiting room for twenty minutes when Jason came running in, "Come and see my daughter! She's the most beautiful baby in the world!"

Andrew held back but Carol and Jason both said, "You too, Andrew!"

They went into the room, and Andrea was holding Jamie Grace. She hadn't been cleaned yet, so Carol didn't ask to hold her, but she leaned over and kissed both her daughter and granddaughter. Andrea's eyes were sparkling.

Carol said, "I don't know how you did this, Andrea. You just had a baby and you look gorgeous. I was in labor with you for about four days and you were in labor for about four minutes."

"Mom, you exaggerate on both counts!"

Andrew spoke up, "Andrea, your mother is right, you do look gorgeous and so does your baby."

The nurse made them leave then so they could finish with Andrea and Jamie Grace. "Andrea, we'll be back in about an hour. We won't stay long. You'll need your rest."

Carol and Andrew walked outside together. Carol was beaming, "Andrew, I want to thank you for being here for me, and for Andrea. I don't know what I would have done without you."

"You don't know how glad I am that I was here, Carol. It meant a lot to me to share this experience with you. I love Andrea like she was my own daughter."

He was watching her closely. She looked up at his face. She saw love and kindness in his eyes. He took her hand and led her to a bench. "Carol, I want to talk to you."

"What is it, Andrew?"

"Carol, I have found myself falling in love with you…I know how you feel...I'm not trying to push you."

Andrew paused and looked into Carol's beautiful green eyes that he loved so much, "I feel that we can have a wonderful future together if you would be willing to give *us* a chance. I care more for you than I thought possible. You make me feel whole. In the time since we met, I have worked to be a better person…not to impress you, but because it felt right. You create in me a desire to be as good as I can be just by being who you are. I know that we are good for each other, and good with each other. Together we can be one...don't worry…I'm not proposing to you…yet."

He paused again and took a deep breath. He took both Carol's hands in his and continued, "Carol, my darling, someday I hope you will allow me to make you my wife. I want to spend the rest of my life making you happy. For now, you will make me the happiest man in the world if you will tell me that you are willing to move forward in this relationship, and that you will allow me to be the only man in your life. Promise me that marriage can be a shared goal for us."

They looked into each other's eyes silently. "Andrew," Carol began, "I believe we can have a beautiful future together. I realize now that every life has many chapters, and in my life I want you in the next chapter."

Andrew took Carol in his arms and they shared a tender yet, passionate kiss.

Whose cake do you like better: Andrea's Cuban Rum Cake, or Angie's Dr Pepper Cake? Here are the recipes so you can try them both...

Andrea's Cuban Rum Cake

Ingredients:
1 18 oz pkg of yellow cake mix
4 eggs
2 tbsp grated lemon peel
1 3oz pkg Jello vanilla pudding
½ cup Bacardi dark rum
½ cup water
½ cup canola cooking oil

Glaze:
4 oz butter
1 cup sugar
½ cup Bacardi rum
¼ cup water
dusting of powdered sugar

Directions:
Preheat oven to 350°. Prepare the cake mix, using a large bowl. Using an electric mixer, first whip the eggs, then add in the yellow cake mix, pudding filling, lemon peel, rum, water and oil. Mix well. Grease and flour the bundt pan, then pour mix into it. Use a 12 cup bundt circular pan. Bake for 1 hour, inserting a skewer in the cake to make sure it is baked thoroughly. Remove cake from oven and let cool.

Glaze - Prepare the glaze by melting butter in a saucepan. Add the sugar, water and rum, and slowly bring to a boil. Then reduce to medium, and let cook for 10 mins. Let cool. Make holes in cake by pricking the top of the cake all over. Slowly pour the glaze all over the cake evenly and let sit for 1 hour to let cake absorb the glaze. Sprinkle powdered sugar on top of cake. Serve using serving plate and enjoy!

** Andrea got this recipe from www.Mejordecuba.com.*

Angie's Dr Pepper Cake

Ingredients:

1 cup butter or margarine (butter is better)
1 cup Dr Pepper
2 cups unsifted all-purpose flour
1 ½ cups sugar
1 tsp cinnamon
1 tsp baking soda
pinch salt
4 tbsp cocoa
2 beaten eggs
2 tsp vanilla
½ cup buttermilk
1 ½ cups miniature marshmallows

Frosting:
½ cup Dr Pepper
¼ cup butter
3 tbsp cocoa
3 cups sugar
½ cup pecans
1 tsp vanilla

Directions:
Melt butter. Add the Dr Pepper and stir well. Mix all of the dry ingredients together in a large mixing bowl. Add the eggs, buttermilk, vanilla and marshmallows. Pour the Dr Pepper mixture over the rest of the ingredients in the mixing bowl. Mix them together well. Bake at 350° in a greased 9x12" pan for 30-35 minutes.

Frost – Heat Dr Pepper, cocoa and butter, but don't bring to a hard boil. Stir in rest of ingredients and mix together well. Spread Dr Pepper frosting on while cake is still hot.
After cake is frosted, put it under the broiler on the top oven rack. Broil for a few seconds only, just until frosting starts to get tiny air bubbles. Watch carefully so as not to burn cake. Let cake cool for about half an hour before eating.

** Angie got this recipe www.drpepper.com.*

** Email me at mybooks64@gmail.com and let me know which cake you like best. I'll email you back and give you the directions for Andrea's Mojitos, and the Grim Reaper that Jason, Carol and Andrew enjoyed on Halloween night.

Made in the USA
Lexington, KY
13 July 2012